UMBRA

Umbra

Fey & Fate Trilogy

ANDREA STANET

Dragonlight Press

Copyright

This is a work of fiction. Names, characters, places, and incidents either are the product of the author's imagination or are used fictitiously. Any resemblance to actual persons, living or dead, events, or locales is entirely coincidental.

First paperback edition April 2023

Book design by Andrea Stanet

ISBN 979-8-9878854-0-6 (paperback)
ISBN 979-8-9878854-1-3 (ebook)

www.dragonlightpress.com

Dedication

For Michael, my own fey king.

Contents

Prologue

A brown-skinned person with long, wild hair sat in the corner of a dusky bar with a couple, the woman of the duo breaking down in tears. Soft rhythm and blues streamed from the jukebox. The bar's patrons, if they noticed the poignant scene at all, ignored it. The counselor leaned forward to pat the woman's knee. Achingly compassionate.

Staring out the penthouse window of his Manhattan office, the king couldn't shake the image of the subject he'd spent the evening observing from the shadows. What he wouldn't do to be on the receiving end of that comforting touch.

A bang behind him forced him out of the memory. He didn't have to turn to know who had disturbed him.

"My lord, where have you been? Stalking the Shifter girl of unknown origin again?"

"*They*. The Shifter goes by they or them. Aren't you the one always telling me to respect their ways in the Waking world, Morgan?"

She sniffed in annoyance. "And how would you know what language *they* use to identify themselves?"

Because I know everything about them. He was prudent enough not to voice this thought.

The king spoke quietly to the reflection in the glass. "It's not your concern what I do with my free time, Morgan."

"As your betrothed queen, I beg to differ."

He sighed. "A decision made when we were adolescents hardly means—"

"I didn't come here to rehash our history, your highness. The Shadow Network has located your missing dagger. It was detected in the Dawn Court."

"You were correct, as always." Now he did turn to smile at her. A twinge pulled at the muscle inside his chest. Morgan's visage hadn't always been so harsh. Had that been his doing, or was the perpetual frown a product of life in general? "That's why you're my right hand in all things."

An icy glare met his expression of esteem and affection. Would things never be simple between them again? "Who have you sent to retrieve it?"

"No one yet. Who do you recommend, my lord? Perhaps your little thiefling for hire."

The acid in her voice and the shine in her eyes infused the king with the impulse to embrace her. But that would only confuse and complicate matters.

"Careful, Morgan. Put away your claws." He pinched the bridge of his nose. "Do whatever you feel is best. You always do." He turned back to gaze, unseeing, into the night.

The door slammed behind him again, and he knew that Morgan was gone.

Chapter 1

Poughkeepsie, NY
Modern Day

A pair of homeless humans huddled in an alley beside an abandoned storefront. They warmed their hands over a trash-can fire, their conversation wafting toward me on a frosty wind.

"Did you see that dude? Lit the fire with his finger."

"Shit man, I don't care if he lit it out his ass. We got heat for the night."

In the Po-town Fringe, few humans—the ones human society doesn't want—coexist with the changelings. Those who do share the community with changelings have better things to worry about than the weirdness around them. Weirdness like me.

Other than the homeless guys, the streets were mostly empty. I patted the pockets of my navy pea coat and those of my jeans—a final check before entering The Cache.

From the threshold of the club, I scanned the Saturday night crowd. I wore my most recognizable persona—oval face, big dark eyes, deep brown complexion, and two French braids almost to my waist. My target—a changeling with the height of an NBA power forward and the girth of a linebacker—leaned against the end of the bar minding his business. More accurately, he was minding his boss's business. Good.

The Cache belonged to Donny, a low-level, changeling mafia boss. In the Fringe, it was either follow his rule or suffer. Most of the changelings in the Fringe preferred him to existing as second-class citizens in the Dreaming, under the thumbs of the stuck-up, full-blooded fey.

Hard rock music pumped from the speakers as I approached the dude. This might be a little more painful than I anticipated.

As I jostled my way through a tightly packed crowd, my foot slipped in what I hoped was just a beer spill. Cigarette smoke, alcohol, and dozens of different perfume scents all assaulted my sinuses.

When I reached Mega Goon, I craned my neck and smiled. "Hey! How's it going up there? Just wondering—I came across some interesting photos. You think Donny's wife might want to know what he was doing last night? Or *who*?" I wiggled my eyebrows.

The lackey lowered his gaze to mine and scowled but gave no other reaction. Still, the press of patrons around us eased as people cleared a circle around us.

Guess we'll be doing this the hard way. Damn.

"Nothing...? Fine." I backhanded him across the jaw.

Now *that* got me a reaction. Within moments, I

was bound with zip-ties, eyes shut, apparently un-conscious. I didn't bother to fight. It didn't suit my purpose.

Like I knew he would, the bouncer made a call from his cell. I could imagine Donny's voice on the other end, *"Throw that bitch in a cage and let 'er stew. I'll show her some photos."* He wasn't the most eloquent guy in the Fringe.

Mega Goon slung me over his shoulder and headed out of the club, undisturbed. Inside, no one had tried to help me. The changelings knew better than to interfere with Donny's boys. I wasn't mad at them.

Dangling upside down, I had to force my body not to shiver in the October air so my captor wouldn't know I was awake. My hands throbbed as I let myself be carried through the dark, deserted streets. Just my beefy bouncer, carting me around like a freaking cave-man. Bizarre shit like this was partly what kept most humans out.

The Fringes give off an energy, a "vibe." To humans, it screams, *Head the other way! This is not for you!* To changelings and some other mythic races, it offers a hearty welcome.

There's no magical glamour created by the change-ling population. Who'd have the time or energy to maintain such a thing? Nope, it's just a simple matter of humans' innate ability to deny, shun, and avoid anything different. Uncomfortable. Other.

Then there are the humans who long for something more than what their mundane, mediocre world has to offer. The dreamers. If not for them, changelings—human and fey half breeds—wouldn't exist. Dreamers wander into the Fringes or the Dreaming, subconsciously seeking novelty. They are perfectly comfortable with strangeness. They embrace otherness.

Finally, MG took me into an old brownstone and down to a ridiculously bright cellar with the two tiny windows covered by steel plates. Another of Donny's thugs dozed behind a wooden desk.

"Yo, newb. Wake up."

The overweight, no-neck guard jerked upright and wiped his chin. "Yeah! The kid's secure. See?" He referred to a crying fey boy locked in one of the two steel cages that occupied most of the room.

MG said, "I got another one for you. Boss said do not take your eyes off her. Not for one second. Not for any reason."

He dropped me into a ratty chair next to the desk and slapped my face a few times. The first one almost took my head off since I couldn't tense up my muscles. That was going to give me a crick. Blood flowed from inside one cheek over my tongue.

The second slap made my ear ring. I moaned, more for the convincing performance than from pain. With the last blow, my head popped upright, and I cried out. "Damn it! What do you want?" My eyes rolled around as if I was dazed. "And it's *them*, not her, you fucking misgendering fascist," I slurred.

"Whatever. You're awake, and I'm done here." MG

left. Somehow, he didn't seem to cherish our time together as much as I had.

The doughy guard yanked me back up to my feet, patted me down, and stripped off my coat. He also relieved me of my tools—daggers, lock picks, a pack of gum, darts, and other assorted goodies.

I sized up Chubby. He was still close to a foot taller than my current 5'8" frame. That was manageable. And it almost guaranteed he'd underestimate me.

He tossed me into the empty cage like yesterday's garbage. The lock clicked into place. A thick chain slid around the cage bars and was secured by a padlock that emitted an eerie red aura.

The guard fell into his chair and plopped his boots up onto the desk. His bulk made the chair legs creak. He closed his eyes and crossed his arms across a paunchy gut that was barely contained by a bullet-proof vest. *That's new. When did they start wearing Kevlar?* Who needed human weapons and armor when they had magic? Who did they think would be shooting?

Donny owned this building too. Under the fluorescent lights, I had noticed a few other new improvements. He had seriously upped his game in the past month since I'd last been here. Where had he gotten the resources for these renovations?

The walls had a new layer of steel over the old concrete. A ring of blue light glowed around the ceiling seams, and a new camera had been installed in the corner diagonal to where I stood, leaning against narrowly spaced cage bars.

I had seen the boy in the adjacent cell a few times around the Fringe. He was barely into his teens. The vampire blood they had drugged him with was probably wearing off. Thankfully, he had stopped crying. As far as I knew, he was the latest guinea pig sold to a vampire prince in the city who was looking to synthesize a fey-blood version of VampX—Ecstasy mixed with vampire blood.

A few paces beyond the guard desk, a shadowy stone stairway led up to a hall where I knew two apartments had been converted into Donny's offices. Between those offices, another set of steps led to the second floor.

He owned several of these buildings and never stayed in any of them for too long. His thugs never knew where or when to expect him. I knew he'd be along soon to inspect the kid.

He'd also probably have one of his goons work me over, just for kicks. Good thing I'm a fast healer.

To try to convince me to work for him, Donny, who could freeze whatever he touched by concentrating on it, occasionally enjoyed chilling parts of my body just before the point of frostbite. If I was in my current female form, he'd put thick iron shackles on super tight so I couldn't shift into a larger, more muscular form. Plus, he was a perv. I pitied his wife being married to such a douche.

If he captured me in a male form, he put me in steel

netting so that shifting smaller wouldn't help. Donny and I did this same pointless dance every once in a while. But I had no interest in the changeling mafia, so he was wasting his time and mine.

From the cage, I continued to scan the room, taking in every new detail until a plan jelled.

Now I could get to work.

Chapter 2

I'd been in the "dungeon," as I called it, nursing bruises and biding my time for about an hour when the cage door clanged. Years ago, I would have been itching to shift, overwhelmed by too much energy and no outlet for it. Now I breathed and waited it out.

I peeked over my shoulder from my position standing next to the rickety bunk bed in the corner of my cell, resting my head in my arms against the top mattress. The bunk shielded a bucket. From the smell, I guessed the pail wasn't empty, but I avoided confirming my suspicion.

The chubby guard shoved in a new cellmate and locked us in together. The new guy beamed at me like it was his birthday. Why would anyone smile about being tossed into a steel cell by a crook-nosed thug?

A ring of keys and a wooden baton landed onto the guard's desk next to the equipment that had been taken from me. I put my head back on my arms.

From behind, I felt a tug on one of my two braids. Without thinking, I dropped toward the floor and swung my leg in an arc. My cellmate jumped over it. *Fast. Impressive.* I drew back my arm to strike.

He dodged again.

"Strange to find a fighter with such long hair," my cellmate said.

In the middle of my next punch, I froze and hoped he didn't notice how I had almost unbalanced myself. It was a matter of professional pride.

Damn. He's good.

He could probably be useful to me, but I didn't want any added responsibility. Better to work alone. That way if I messed up, I had no one to blame but me.

"Sorry if I startled you, but the oddness of your hair compelled me to touch it."

The oddness of his statement compelled me to respond. "What?"

"Your hair. Rare, considering your profession. Your lack of ear-piercing panic suggests you work for Rebus, the Fringe's own Robin Hood and mercenary agent. Correct?" My cellmate's voice was deep and silky. A bright grin suggested a high degree of self-satisfaction.

"Wrong. I work for myself, and I work alone." Telling other people what to do and trying to think for them could lead to trouble. I relaxed my stance and shook out my fists. "Let me get this straight. Since, by your account, I'm a thief with hair you perceive to be unusually long, you get a free pass to touch me?"

"I apologized."

Having to deal with a psycho today didn't factor into my plans.

My focus shifted away from him, but he continued. "It's easy to grab and stands out. Makes you noticeable."

"You must not be from around here. Black females with long braids are pretty common."

"You're right of course. It must be that you, yourself, are just... striking."

That earned him an eyeroll. After climbing to the top bunk where I had a better view of the dungeon, I glanced back at the newcomer, considered explaining, and then changed my mind. Thugs and molesters I could handle, but it was always better to avoid crazies, especially in the Fringe.

I examined his features now: Tall and wiry—over six feet, olive skin, and dark eyes heavily rimmed with black eyeliner. Wavy, black layers hung over his forehead and past his shoulders to frame his face. A couple of years older than me. Twenty-four? He dressed in a high-end-trendy style—black velvet choker, fishnet half shirt, and two hundred dollar jeans that were ripped just so. The fashion choice was interesting. It worked for him.

Finally, my gaze landed on something that could identify this guy. Pointed ears hidden by his hair. Aside from the intangible energy signature he gave off, the ears were the telltale sign of a fey. Probably full-blooded since changeling ears were a little more rounded, closer to their human side. The awkwardness and incomplete knowledge of human ways would have been a giveaway if I had been paying closer attention.

What was a fey doing in the dungeon?

I pushed aside the question of why he had been snagged. It wasn't my business.

Sitting cross-legged on the thin mattress, decrepit springs digging into my butt, I reached up with my left hand toward the blue light and along the edge of the ceiling.

A zap rocked me back and sent a jolt up my arm. I grunted. The tips of my fingers were charred and stung as if I'd reached into a wasp nest. A scowl twisted my mouth as I processed the setback and climbed down to the bottom bunk. Leaning forward, elbows on knees, I worked out my next steps.

"I thought that looked like some sort of lightning spell ward."

Please go away. I don't have time for this. He did not go away.

"So, what are you in for?" he said.

"Better question: are you stupid?"

"I can't stand to see a damsel in distress." He towered over me with a smirk and leaned down to whisper in my ear. "I can get us out of here."

I laughed. "For a price, I'm sure, fey. And assuming that I'm a damsel is sexist and offensive. No thanks. I'm fine."

He grinned wickedly. "I can see that from your fingers. Good to meet you, *Fine*—person in need of a more practical hair style. I'm...Dúl, now that you ask."

"As in you're challenging me to a duel, or as in split personality?"

"Yes." He stuck a hand forward as if to shake.

I stared, waiting, and when he didn't move, I finally clasped it.

"Do you still refuse my offer to get us both out of here?"

"Yes. Now, please go away. I'm trying to concentrate."

Dúl held up his hands, palms out in mock defeat, and reclined against the bunks. He watched me. I tried to ignore him, but the intensity of his gaze unnerved me. With a deep breath, I forced myself to brush aside the chill at the back of my neck and to focus on the issue at hand—getting out of this cell.

Time for plan B. I went around the bunk to the smelly piss pot, held my breath, and crouched out of sight of the camera.

Unfortunately, when I let them capture me, the guard patted me down and took my coat with most of my tools. This left me in a snug pair of low-rise black jeans and a black tank top—not many places to hide anything.

I reached into my left braid and withdrew a few three-inch-long picks wrapped in a length of fishing line. These were always somewhere on my body because I never knew when a string would come in handy—like right now.

"Ah. Now I see the reason for the hair," Dúl muttered. "And when I touched it, you—"

"Shut up!" I peeked at the guard to see if he stirred. "I wear my hair this long when I feel like it. And sometimes I don't. I go with whatever suits me in the moment." That wasn't true, strictly speaking. Sometimes circumstances forced me into one body or another. But he didn't need to know that.

My scalp tingled as I withdrew all the hair inward. As they slithered out of sight, the ends of my braids tickled my shoulders until only a thin coating of hair covered my skull.

"Happy?" I hissed.

Dúl tilted his head to one side. His eyes twinkled as his gaze travelled over my body from head to toe. "I have to say, the long hair is lovely, but this look has its own appeal…"

I huffed, turned my back to him, unwound the picks, and regrew my braids. Next, I tied one end of the fishing line to the center of my titanium pick and meandered to the corner of the cell nearest the guard's desk. Keeping my back to the camera, I poked my hands through the bars as far as I could, not even all the way to my elbows. My hands clasped together, and my forehead rested against the cold steel of my prison.

With a little sleight of hand, I positioned the pick between my right thumb and middle finger and the string around my left index finger. I aimed through one eye and whispered a command. "Claw."

The tiniest flick of my fingers shot the pick across the ten feet between my pack of gum over on the desk and me. The pick glowed purple, curved at the ends, and clutched the object I needed.

So far, so good.

Barely moving my fingers, I slowly gathered the line back into my left hand, drawing the gum closer to the edge of the desk. When it went over the side and smacked into the floor, I winced and stilled.

The guard snorted and began to snore. Not wanting to take any chances in case he was only faking sleep, I continued at a slow pace. It seemed to take a decade, but the gum was finally in my hands.

It wasn't exactly gum, as in the chewing kind, although it was packaged to look like spearmint flavor of a human brand. Rebus had acquired the resin of some special tree in the Dreaming and worked his own magic on it. My adopted father was probably behind his bar, sliding a pint of brew down to one of the Saturday night regulars. I sighed deeply for the camera and lay down on the bottom bunk facing away from my audience.

Dúl muttered, "This ought to be interesting," and climbed up to the top bunk, crunching his lanky torso down probably to avoid whacking his head. Thank goodness he seemed inclined to leave me alone now. The springs above me squeaked with each of his movements, and then the only sounds were the guard's piggy sleep noises and the teenager's occasional whimpers.

I pulled a stick of the green gum from the pack and stuck it in my mouth. As I chewed, it grew to a wad bigger than a jumbo jawbreaker. Turning over as if restless, I glimpsed toward the camera to measure the distance between it and the corner of the cell nearest to it. It was far—at least twenty-five feet. The shot would be nearly impossible. So nice to have an adopted father with a specialty for enchanting thieves' tools.

Getting up, I began to pace the room, running my hand over my face to slip the gum into my palm. When I reached the corner of the cell, I poked my arms through again. After taking a few seconds to aim, I tossed the wad in an upward arc. It flew and covered the camera lens with a muffled splat.

I grinned to myself and then caught Dúl staring at me with a lopsided smile. "Impressive, but don't you think they'll get suspicious when there's no video from this room?"

Some people always have to rain on others' parades. "I'll worry about that later."

He shrugged.

Now I had to move quickly because as much as I hated to admit it, he was right.

The cell door had a normal lock, but the new padlock was a problem.

The urge to ask Dúl what he thought about the magic on the lock crossed my mind. He was a fey, and likely knew more about magic than I did, but I rejected the notion. No need to involve him in my scheme.

The titanium pick had straightened itself out. I gripped it between my thumb and forefinger and wriggled it in the cell-door's deadbolt. Both shimmered and glowed purple. I smiled when the lock opened with a muffled click. That was the easy part—it was enchanted to be able to open any mundane lock.

Now on to the padlock. I didn't like that red light around it.

As soon as the pick, my favorite, touched the red aura, there was a quiet poof, and the pick disintegrated in my hands. I snarled at the chain and mentally cursed Donny. "Damn it!"

Whispered words reached me from the top bunk. "Anti-magic. I hope you've got another one of those."

My response was a low growl. These magical wards had to come from a first-generation changeling, as close as one could get to being fullblood, or from some underground connection to the Dreaming. Either way, it meant big bucks. What was Donny involved in that would gain him that type of capital?

This was taking too long. I should have been out and on my way already. Resisting the temptation to kick the bars, I focused. If the lock had an anti-magic ward on it, I should be able to pick it the old-fashioned way.

I crossed the cell to the bottom bunk and grabbed my two other picks—plain, old, and iron. My first ones. No magic. All they needed was a steady, sensitive hand.

After poking them into the lock's mouth, I shifted them around the lock's guts until I felt the slightest give and heard a tiny click.

Murmuring a silent prayer, I quietly removed the chain from the bars, placed it on the bed, and eased the cell door open. I expected the creak that sounded. The guard still didn't move. Faking sleep?

My senses were all on high alert now, taking in everything at once, as if time had slowed. I inched the door wide enough to squeeze my body through. Patches of grayish-green were speckled with black mold across the concrete floor. I darted to the stairs on silent feet.

My skin crawled as I dodged a spider web up in the threshold. Light peeked into the stairway. I pressed against the wall into welcoming shadows.

The guard grunted. I heard movement.

"What the—" Then the guard roared, "Sonofabitch! Where's she at?"

The bunk bed springs squeaked. I heard a yawn.

"Huh?" Dúl said. The silky quality had lcft his voice. His whine was boyish. "I dunno. I fell asleep. Not exactly a party in here."

The guard cursed. The cell door banged shut. What a shame. I would have let Dúl escape once I was finished here.

There were three clomping footsteps, shuffling objects, more curses, and whimpers from the boy. *Damn.*

I called to mind everything I remembered about one of the guards I had encountered when they picked me up. Holding the image in my mind, I began to change.

My skin prickled. A chill flowed through me as if cool liquid trickled over my head and down my back while fabric absorbed into my flesh. Skin stretched and writhed. Bones and muscles softened like taffy and reformed into larger, thicker shapes. Finally, I patted my hands over myself to do a last check that I hadn't forgotten to change an ear or left my tank top on instead of creating the illusion of a bullet-proof vest.

Shapeshifting was my nature, but Rebus taught me to always check twice and act once.

Back in the dungeon, it sounded like the guard was ransacking the place to find me and that he was forcing Dúl into the cell with the kid. Convenient.

Satisfied that I hadn't forgotten any minor details, I opened the door at the top of the stairs, let it slam, thudded down the steps, and called out.

"Hey! Hope you got that kid ready! Boss is on his way to inspect him!"

I took my time, laughing inside at the creative curses the guard spat. I almost pitied him. I would have been shitting my pants, too, if I were in his position. Then again, I doubt I would have been dumb enough to take a nap after being warned not to take my eyes off someone.

When I was a few steps from the bottom, the room quieted. I clomped down the last stairs. The guard's back was to me as he inspected the lock on the cell door.

"Uh, who did you say you were picking up, again?" he said, his voice gnarled and suspicious.

Uh oh. "Kendal. The kid."

He turned toward me. "Right. Password?"

Shit. Why can't anything be easy?

When Kendal's parents hired me to rescue him, I had planned to get him out without any conversations. I'd have to wing it.

"Damn. Boss just told it to me not an hour ago." I pointed to my forehead. "Bad short-term memory."

"You—"

I charged. In an instant, the goon had his baton in hand. He swung it up toward my jaw. This big body, nearly seven feet tall, was bulky—not as agile as my previous frame. I leaned back. The baton cracked against my chin. Before the guard could bring it down on my head, I grabbed his wrist and elbowed him in the nose.

I jabbed my two first fingers into his eyes. He howled. Swiping his baton, I whacked him across the knees. He sank. I batted the back of his skull twice. He fell over, unconscious.

A longer fight to get a better feel for this particular body in action would have been fun, but I had a changeling to rescue.

After grabbing my gear and the keys, I opened the corner cell. Once I freed the occupants, I moved toward the kid who looked confused and lost. "Come on, Kendal."

He shrank away from me.

"It's okay. Your parents sent me for you. We have to go—now."

"Even if you had known the password, it was the voice that gave you away." Dúl hadn't left.

I turned. "What?"

"That's how the guard knew. You needed to make your voice more gravelly. Throw in a grunt or two."

Beginner mistake. If I'd had the time, I would have mentally kicked myself for getting distracted. "Thanks." Why *was* I so distracted?

Kendal had settled down and seemed to realize I wasn't one of his captors. I towed him by the arm out of the cell. "Hang on," I said.

I stomped over the thug's body. After grabbing the rest of my things, I borrowed a pair of handcuffs, stripped off his vest, and cuffed his hands to the cell bars. I considered shifting forms, then rejected the idea. Being disguised in this beefed-up body might be useful, especially if we had to fight our way out. Plus, if it were injured, shifting back later would speed up the healing process.

When I fitted the vest onto Kendal, it swallowed the poor boy's skinny frame. Before I could tell him to follow me, I spotted Dúl waiting by the stairs.

"You don't want to be associated with this if any-one sees us."

"And miss any action? Not a chance."

He was persistent. Like a rash.

"Whatever." I sighed, turning to Kendal. "Stay close to me."

From the pocket of my jacket, I retrieved a small black talisman with a rune carved into it that I had received from an old changeling in exchange for dragging her addict son out of a vamp den a while back. Easing the door open a crack, I held the stone to my lips and whispered, "Sleep." I then flicked it into the room, counted to ten, and hoped it worked.

Tiny sconces on each side of the hall cast dim illumination along the walls. I sneaked into the hall and saw that the two guards were passed out on the ground. The office doors were open, and they appeared to be empty. Voices and laughter carried down from the second floor. I waved my two companions forward. We reached the end of the staircase.

A shot rang out. Searing pain sliced through my shoulder as a bullet grazed me. A bullet! The bastards were shooting at us from the landing. And I looked like one of them—the morons.

"Run!" I shoved Kendal toward the outer door. Spinning to face the guards, I plucked another stone from my pocket and hurled it at the wall to my right.

It exploded. A thick, white cloud filled the hall. I ran out, slamming the door behind me, thankful that it had been unlocked. And no wonder—they had guns. I couldn't believe it. Who uses human weapons when they have magic? That was cheating.

Angry, I snatched an old supermarket receipt and a pen from my pockets and scribbled on the back.

Guns? BS, Don!
Never yours,
Merc

I stabbed a dagger through it, pinning it to the door. With a gesture toward Kendal and Dúl, I reluctantly led them into the night.

Chapter 3

We moved fast down side streets and back streets until we reached the parking lot for the Over-Hudson Span. After skirting through the bushes, down a hill, and across a few private backyards, we reached the river's edge and followed it south. Back up another part of the hill, we found a deserted section of train tracks shielded by scraggly trees.

Once we stopped, I searched through my pockets for something to stop the bleeding in my shoulder. *Bastards ruined my favorite coat.* I had nothing and was about to cut off the leg of my jeans when a handkerchief was waved in front of my face.

Since I had just freed Dúl from the dungeon, I figured it was okay to accept it from him. The wound was minor, and the bleeding stopped quickly. I shuddered to think how much worse that could have turned out but put those thoughts out of my mind just as fast as they entered. I could process all this new information later.

While we waited for Kendal's parents to meet us where we had previously agreed, I shifted back to one of my two preferred forms—the one I had been wearing when I was "detained." Because of the pain my change would take a little extra mental energy to achieve but would speed up the healing in my shoulder. Plus, I just wanted to lose this goon's body and take back my own.

When I wore a female form, it usually leaned towards androgynous—small chest and narrow hips with muscular legs. I liked bigger boobs sometimes, but they often got in my way, so I saved them for private times or those moments when I needed to cause a distraction. My one indulgence in this shape was dark, kinky hair almost to my waist. Most of the time, it was in two braids, but sometimes, I loved to let it go wild.

My male form was similar with stronger features in the face, slightly taller height, and ropy upper-body muscles. In that one, I would go almost bald or grow out my curls to shoulder-length. These days my choice of form usually depended on how I felt any given day and what would work best for whatever situation I was heading into.

When I was younger and in school, I would have to stay in one body no matter how I felt, so I got used to sticking to one form. It wasn't like I could show up as a boy claiming to be the same person. It was fine being a girl, most of the time.

After I shifted, Kendal huddled to my right on the riverbank and shivered.

"Sorry, kid. I didn't know we'd be in the Wild West back there."

"Just cold. Why are we here? You handing me over to the Vamps after all?"

"What? No! To your parents."

He digested that, pulling his arms inside the vest. "Um, thanks. For getting me out of there. Don't know how they got me. I was careful."

That was a good question. The obvious answer was that another changeling snitched to get out of their own debt to Donny. Kendal's parents had owed money to one of Donny's businesses—I hadn't asked for too many details—but they would have hidden Kendal's existence. Right now, the kid didn't need to think about who might have betrayed him and his family. He'd been through enough.

I kept my expression blank. "Don't thank me. It was just business."

He nodded. "Can I..." Kendal gestured toward a copse of bushes.

"Yeah, go on. Just try to keep it quiet, okay?"

He slunk away. The vamps would have destroyed this quiet kid in a matter of weeks, and his parents had known it. The cost might break them, but they insisted on hiring me. Everyone knew I was glad to save someone from the vampires. I had my reasons.

"So...Merc? Interesting name." I had thought Dúl might take the hint and leave on his own, but clearly, he wanted something. I hoped he would get to the point quickly. Once I was done here, he had to go.

"You read over my shoulder before. Rude."

"You weren't exactly hiding. Is it short for mercenary, or is it a play on 'murky?'"

"Yes," I said and forced myself not to snicker. It was harder not to smile than it had been with Kendal. I sensed Dúl was doing the same. "Why are you still here? If you plan to follow me for the rest of the night, I should tell you that my boyfriend won't appreciate it."

Dúl nodded. "Why don't you complete your transaction, and then we can talk. I have a proposition for you." When I opened my mouth to protest, he quickly clarified, "A business proposition."

Before I could respond, Kendal trotted out of the bushes. I envied him. Even at fifteen, he knew who and what he was. He hunkered next to me and closed his eyes.

A few seconds later, crunching leaves in the otherwise silent night alerted us that someone approached. Two shadowy figures appeared from the brush. Kendal's parents followed the same path we had. He perked up and bounded toward them. He nearly tackled his mother. She hugged him, struggling to balance, laughing, and weeping at once.

Kendal's father, Drew, rushed toward me. The front toe of one of his boots flapped with each step. I stood to meet him. He reached his hands forward and shook mine fervently. Dúl hung back.

"Thank you so much, Merc. Rebus said you'd get our boy. We can never repay you."

I hated this part.

"I was happy to help. What will you do now, though? He's on Donny's radar. They might come after him again. Donny doesn't like to lose face. Or money."

Drew released my hands and began to wring his own. His wool jacket was frayed and shabby with mismatched buttons. A day or two worth of scruff covered his cheeks.

"No idea. We'll head across the river. Highland, then up north. Karina's got some folks up that way. They'll help us get over into the Winter Court. Start fresh. Too many vamps comin' up to Poughkeepsie from the City."

I had to agree with him there. A cool wind kicked up, and a couple of flurries began to fall.

What the hell? October's too early for snow. I crossed my arms in front of my chest.

"You all should get gone then. Good luck." I hoped he would take the hint and leave, but he reached into his pocket. "Listen, keep your money. Truly. You're going to need it."

"Rebus said you might not want to take your due. But we have to give you something." Drew held out a bronze wrist cuff with a clear, faceted crystal in the center. "Please. Take this."

"You should hold onto it. You could sell it if you run short—"

"It's enchanted." He pressed the cuff into my hands. "Speak the word *Dekrar*, and three duplicates of you will appear. They'll act independently unless you're hit or you banish them. Comes in handy if you need to confuse an enemy."

My mouth dropped open. This was an amazing gift for these people to part with. I really wanted it but felt a little guilty taking something so valuable from someone who needed it much more than I did.

Kendal turned to wave at me. A grin stretched across his face as he nuzzled against his mother's side. She brushed tears from her face before waving and leading him away.

"Please, Merc. This is nothing compared to what you've returned to us. We insist."

I sighed, nodded, and shook his hand. "Thanks. I'll use it well. And if you ever need me—"

"We know how to contact you. Thank you."

He trotted after his family, leaving me holding the bracelet. I put it on and stared at it for a moment. It wasn't that I had a problem taking money for jobs, but I had a soft spot for changeling kids, and a special hatred of vamps. Sometimes it felt wrong getting paid for something I'd do for free. But I was working on it. As Paris, my boyfriend, often reminded me, we had to eat.

"Declining money? You are an intriguing mercenary, murky one."

I had forgotten about Dúl. Somehow, I thought he'd intended me to do so.

"I don't reject monetary payment from everyone. You, for example, would have to make one hell of an offer for my services. You can tell me about your proposition on the way back."

We climbed the bank, crossed the train tracks, and headed toward Rebus's place. My adopted father was a Canadian changeling. To my understanding, he had been part of the Winter Queen's intelligence service. Maybe one day he would tell me exactly what he had done for her frosty majesty, but these days, he owned a neighborhood bar and lived above it.

Up until a couple of years ago, I had lived there, too, with him and his wife, Natalie, a Summer changeling whose family had migrated across the river generations ago. Rebus and Nat had rescued me off the streets when I was around seven. Reportedly, I had just appeared in the Fringe one day. I remembered almost nothing about my parents or any other family I may have had.

I sometimes dreamt of a woman singing lullabies in a Spanish-sounding language. I also recalled being held in big, rough hands. The scents of orchid and cigars always seemed to tug at my heartstrings, but I couldn't summon up my parents' images at all.

For that matter, I didn't remember my *own* original form.

Paris and I now lived a few blocks away from the bar in a building near the City Center Convention Hall. I needed to get rid of Dúl before Paris decided to search the neighborhood for me.

"So," I said to Dúl. "Tell me about the job."

"It's perfect for you. You see, I must confess, I'm

quite familiar with your work. The Shadow Network has quietly raved about you for years. To be honest, I had arranged to be detained by Donny's men the next time you were. I wanted to see you in action for myself."

I stopped walking. So did he.

The night was almost moonless, but a streetlamp lit a small circle of yellow on the pavement. Dúl and I stood outside the range of illumination. In the silence, flurries tickled my nose and eyelashes. A sudden dip in temperature suggested that dawn was close. It occurred to me that maybe I *should* let Paris get at this jerk. But that would have its own price, not to mention that it would be bad for business.

I cleared my throat. "You know, most people who want to know about me just go to Rebus. Lying and spying? Not the best way to start a transaction."

"If you knew who we were up front, you might have passed on the offer without hearing me out."

My shoulders tensed. There were only a few groups I adamantly avoided. This couldn't be good. I started walking again. Dúl followed. Rebus's was a block and a half away.

"On the surface, the job is a simple recovery. But, for political reasons, we can't have our own people directly involved. We will, however, cover all expenses and are prepared to pay generously."

This all-business attitude was another side of Dúl. How many were there?

"Politics and lies—you must be from the Courts."

He smirked. I didn't like working with fullbloods.

Sometimes it seemed like a nice deal to have the stability that came from swearing allegiance to a Court, but once in, there was no getting out. I preferred flexibility and freedom.

"If you know my reputation, you know the Winter Court already tried and failed to recruit me. Why not go to someone friendlier toward your kind?"

"What do you know about the Courts?"

"Enough to know you're always fighting each other, and you're basically manipulative jerks."

That earned me a laugh. "Fair assessment. What if I promise full honesty from here on out?"

I shrugged then stopped walking. We had reached the bar. Muffled music mixed with voices and laughter. "Go on."

"As you probably know, the Dawn and Shadow Courts have been fighting for as long as anyone can remember. Orion, the Dawning Lord, has detained the Shadow Lord's lieutenant, Morgan. He denies any wrongdoing. Since the self-righteous asshat presents himself to be all *noble* and *upstanding*..." Dúl sneered at each word and looked like he wanted to spit. "...no one can implicate him. His sister, the Summer Queen, believes him, and the Winter Queen couldn't care less. She won't get involved unless the Shadow Lord himself is taken."

I stared at Dúl. While his face was clear and calm, he had balled up his fists.

"Wow, you almost look like you want to go after Orion yourself and to hell with anything else."

"So you can see," he continued, ignoring my comment, "that to get Morgan home, we need someone to steal her back. Will you help?"

Something sounded much more personal here than Dúl was letting on, but I wasn't about to pry. It was none of my business. Compensation was.

I had to remind myself that Dúl had already been less than honest. He might be withholding information now.

"Say I was willing to take this on. What are you offering?"

"Name your price. And you can have as large a team—"

"No team."

Calculations raced through my brain. What figure would be worth my while when this job came back to bite me in the ass later? Because it most definitely would.

So many possibilities. I could charge enough to get out of the Fringe. Maybe I wouldn't go as far as New York City, but I could find a nicer place than I had now, something across the river. Get Paris away from temptation. I'd still be close enough to do my work... close to Rebus and Nat.

"Twenty grand, human currency."

"Done."

No hesitation. Wow.

"One small caveat—I hope it won't be an issue. I'll be tagging along part of the way."

And the trouble begins. "I'll get back to you."

Chapter 4

For a few minutes after Dúl left, I faced the street from the bar's doorway, relishing the silence and envisioning what I could do with my commission if I took this job.

A pair of hands snaked around my hips. Tanned, tattooed arms squeezed, and straight teeth nipped the back of my neck. I shut my eyes and breathed in deeply, filling my nostrils with the scents of musky soap and mint. Some post-job loving would be a perfect way to end the night.

Paris sucked hard on my skin and grinded against my ass. I moaned. Wriggling out of his grasp, I turned to face him and wrapped my arms around his waist.

"You could just say hi," I said through a smile. I stood on tip toes to kiss the corner of his mouth.

"Hi. How'd it go with the kid? D'you get paid?"

My smile disintegrated. Money was all he seemed to care about lately. Almost all he cared about.

His eyes twitched. His black hair was wet and spiked as if he had just showered. When I got home,

I'd probably find sweat-soaked clothes on the bathroom floor.

"I'm fine," I said slowly. "Bullet graze and a couple of bruises. Thanks for asking."

He huffed and pulled away. "Another freebie, Merc? We talked about this."

"The way I remember it, you yelled, and I graciously listened. Those people needed what cash they had."

I started to skirt around him toward the bar door.

"And we don't need cash?" Paris grabbed my arm. Hard. I winced. His changeling side gave him enhanced strength. Sometimes he forgot. He never used to. Would he be so forgetful if I had a bigger body? Funny how these days he complained when I stayed in my male form around him.

Paris and I met in Poughkeepsie Community College's Criminal Justice program. We had gone into the major for opposite reasons, but we hit it off right away. It helped that I recognized his subtle changeling traits. When we sparred in martial arts, he had above average strength, and his skin was slightly tougher than a human's.

He had bad-boy good looks, the brains of a total geek, a passion for creating impenetrable security systems, and big dreams of working for RavCorp. I fell hard. For the first year, we were swept into our own private world. When necessity—his—had us searching the classifieds for apartments together, my family wasn't happy.

At that point, the big reveals came—about my

"work" for Rebus and my shifting ability. I was afraid Paris would freak out. He had found it sexy at first.

Not so much the day I had come out of the shower in my male form. He literally fell backward onto the bed like I was some knife-wielding serial killer. "What the fuck, Merc? Are you going on a job you forgot to tell me about?"

"What's wrong? I shapeshift. Some days, I just feel like this body suits me better. You don't have an issue when I change into different female shapes."

"That's different." He was covering his eyes, as if he'd never been in a shower room with other dicks around. "That's like being able to fuck a million different girls without cheating. This is—can you change back, please? Or put on a towel?"

I switched to female and from then on only wore a male body when I was on a job that called for it or when I was at home with Rebus and Nat. It wasn't too much worse than being in school. I didn't want Paris to feel uncomfortable, or worse, not to be attracted to me.

His reaction back then should have been a sign. Maybe it had been, and I was just blinded by love at the time.

Now his narrow, black eyes flashed accusations at me. "We had a plan. How are we supposed to make it happen with you refusing money all the time?" He sneered.

I grew bigger for a second, just long enough to tower over him and yank my arm out of his grasp. "I bring in more than my share, and the bills are always covered." We also had some extra money squirreled away that he didn't know about. I had started putting it away to surprise him so he could transfer to a school in NYC and finish his bachelors. I shrank back down to normal.

I poked him in the chest. "You're just mad because you were hoping to score some more X. What happened? Burned through your whole secret stash already?" Being smaller didn't mean I had to put up with his aggression. "Keep handling me like that and you'll be making plans by your damned self."

"Come on, Merc.·I told you, I'm clean."

Liar. There was no point in calling him on it. He'd just deny he'd had any tonight. When I crossed my arms in front of my chest, he tried a different approach.

"I thought the plan was to get out of the Fringe. You and me. Go someplace where there are opportunities for both of us." He stroked one cheek, letting his fingers trail down the side of my neck. He knew my weaknesses. "Don't you still want that? Want me?"

I sighed. "Of course I do. But where are we rushing off to? We can't even agree on a location yet. What we have is a goal, but not a plan—not yet. I *do* want it, I swear. So, we'll keep working on it." *And I'll keep working on getting you clean.* "It'll come together. I promise."

Apparently, he didn't like my answer. When I tried

to snuggle up to him again, he shoved his hands into his pants pockets. It felt like rejection.

"What'd they give you this time, anyway? Something valuable at least, or some bullshit like McDonald's coupons?"

I could have mentioned the wrist cuff in my pocket or the new job offer to appease him. Instead, I stepped away from him and opened the bar door.

"Asshole." I went inside.

He didn't follow.

Inside the almost-empty bar, Rebus was wiping down the counter. An ancient jukebox was shut down for the night, but a small radio, nestled between a mirror behind the bar and the cash register, wailed out a soft-rock tune. Glasses clinked as Nat cleared them from the dark wood tables. She swept shoe dirt, pistachio shells, and other food debris into a standing dustpan.

Rebus didn't look up when the bell over the door clanged. He filled a highball glass with ginger ale and slid it toward me. I gripped the glass hard, still angry at Paris but not wanting Rebus to see that.

"That was quick. Didn't expect to see you 'til after daybreak at least. Your boyfriend gave up hanging around."

"Saw him." I sipped my drink. Now that I wasn't occupied, my shoulder burned and throbbed. "Got the kid out okay but ran into a little problem." Shrugging out of my coat, I pulled off the red-stained cloth. "Got anything for gunshot wounds?"

The bald patch on top of his head, ringed by salt and pepper curls, reflected the bar lights as he cursed, dropped his rag, and hurried around to check my injury. After he glanced toward Nat, her footsteps pounded toward the back office where they kept the first-aid kit.

"What the hell happened out there? Don's guys never use weapons." Rebus examined the graze closer. "Bleeding's stopped. Lucky it wasn't worse."

Nat came back and stroked my hair as he pulled a bottle of betadine out of a red box. I gritted my teeth to hold back a groan when it felt like a blaze erupted in my shoulder. Sweat broke out on my forehead and top lip. Rebus blew on the gash after each dose of betadine, just like he had when I was little. It never really helped then, either, but the attention and attempt to be comforting did.

Once he applied antibiotic ointment and gauze, he picked up his rag and went back to what he had been doing. I refilled my drink.

"The guards were wearing bulletproof vests. I wonder where all the equipment came from? Vamps?"

"Doesn't sound like them. I'll look into in and let you know what I find. Does your boyfriend know you got hurt?" His eyes flicked toward me for a second.

"I told him. He was kind of pissed that I didn't get paid in cash. But the kid's parents gave me an enchanted bracelet that should come in handy." I pulled it from my pocket and walked over to show him.

He turned it over in his hand a couple of times before giving it back. "Nice. I'm guessing that's why dumb ass didn't come in with you?"

Discussing Paris with Rebus was about as fun and productive as slamming myself in the head with a hammer. Protective of me, he had little sympathy toward my drug-addicted other half. He wasn't too keen on me not being able to be totally comfortable in whatever skin I wanted, in my own home, and around the person who was supposed to love all of me. I had convinced myself that Paris would come around eventually. Getting him clean was the priority.

"So...a funny thing happened on my way out of the dungeon...." After recounting all the evening's events, I told Rebus about Dúl's offer.

"Thought you hated all things fullblood."

"I don't hate them. I just find the idea of being stuck in one Court forever... stifling."

"A person's got to keep their options open, right?" Nat chimed in. Picking up a tub of dirty glasses, she grinned, wiggled her wide hips, tossed her long auburn hair, and dramatically exited through the bat-wing doors to the kitchen.

From behind wire-rimmed glasses, Rebus rolled his eyes but smiled.

I agreed with Natalie's general philosophy. She had been with Rebus nearly twice as long as I'd been with the two of them. Words were meaningless. Promises could be broken. From watching my family, the *act* of choosing to stay put, day after day, meant more to me.

"Anyway," I said. "Feelings about the Courts aside, how could I turn down this much money? Paris and me could get set up almost anywhere with that kind of boost."

"Paris and you." He paused. "Anywhere like the city, also known as VampX capital of the world? Are you sure that's the best thing?"

A song with a jazzy bass line came on the radio. Rebus dusted the liquor bottles against the wall mirror, his back to me. His reflection watched my reaction.

"I don't know, Reeb. Can't seem to settle on one thing. But my gut tells me that this thing with the fullbloods could be important for me."

His eyes, reflected in the mirror, found mine. "I've always told you, follow your instincts. If you think there's a real opportunity here, don't let anything—or anyone—hold you back from it. Whatever you decide to do, just be happy."

I peered into my glass, leaned my good arm on the counter, and tapped my toes on the floor. I always felt squirmy when Rebus got all sappy.

Taking a last swig of soda, I brought the glass to the kitchen. We all finished the cleanup together since it might be a while until I saw them again. Near dawn, I finally reached my apartment. Paris was still out. He hadn't been home all night or the previous day, which unfortunately, wasn't that uncommon. There had been many weird events since we got together.

Two years ago, I had thought it strange that after we had been together for almost a year, I hadn't been to Paris's home or met his dad. His mom, an ex-FBI agent injured in the line of duty, had died of a painkiller overdose when he was a baby. His dad, a changeling from Cleveland, remarried when Paris graduated from high school. That was all I knew.

A little curious, and let's face it, a lot immature, I decided to surprise him on our first anniversary. In a deep purple minidress that showed off every curve I sprouted, halter topped with the back plunging to my hips, I showed up at the address that came up when Rebus background checked Paris during our first date. Dead grass, rusted kid toys, and overflowing garbage bins surrounded the Cape Cod with its faded blue paint and ripped screens. A loud argument raged inside.

Brain gears finally kicking into action, I turned to leave as fast as I could. It wasn't fast enough. The door flew open, and Paris stormed out. His scraped knuckles bled. A bright red welt bloomed next to one eye. He stopped short when he saw me. Our eyes locked, pure rage spewing out of his gaze.

"The fuck you doing here?" he roared.

I stumbled back a step. He had never shouted at me before.

"I...It's..." I shrugged and with one limp hand held out a teddy bear and balloons. "I'm so sorry."

"Get out of here, Merc. You shouldn't have come. I'll see you later." He brushed past me, stomped down from the broken concrete step, and jogged up the block.

I glanced over my shoulder once before heading away from the shouting still going on inside.

Later that evening, with a bouquet of daisies and a box of Cap'n Crunch—my guilty pleasure—Paris showed up at the bar. "Didn't you think there was a reason I never brought you home? I didn't want you to see how I lived. My dad's a drunk, and his so-called wife is probably only a couple years older than me. Fucking meth-head waste of space. Bitch tried to pawn my laptop. Again."

"I'm sorry, babe. I had no idea. Can you maybe look for a place of your own?"

He huffed a sarcastic laugh. "Yeah, right. Stocking shelves for Best Buy wouldn't pay for school and a room, forget an apartment."

And so, a plan was hatched. He quit his job at Best Buy and started bouncing nights at Rebus's. I had my "work" and some money saved. Within a month, we had moved in together. That was when the real fun started.

Dusk fell. I taped a brief note to the refrigerator and called Dúl.

~*~

Dressed more elegantly than the previous night, he met me outside the bar. He got out of the back of the limo and came right to me, no hesitation. "Hello, Merc. I was delighted that you accepted my offer." He held out a hand to shake, and when I clasped it, his grip was firm but not obnoxious. He wore a long trench and shiny black boots. A gray silk scarf draped around his neck and down his chest, untied. His top two buttons were open, and his hair was slicked back into a handsome ponytail.

When I had woken up from a too-short nap, I felt like I needed to be in my male body. Like the female body couldn't contain the agitation coursing through me. And maybe a small part of me wanted to test Dúl. Maybe I wanted to be taken seriously by him. He didn't even flinch.

I chose black skinny jeans tucked into ankle boots with a scarlet wool coat over a snug, charcoal crew-neck sweater. Bright red curls were trapped at the back of my head in a neat man-bun. How funny that both Dúl and I had pulled our hair back today. Chunky red glasses completed my look. I carried a change of clothes and my tools in a sleek black tote. I could pass for the devil and felt a little like one.

It was late morning, sunny with a nip in the air. A few people waited at the bus stop on the corner, but otherwise, the street was still sleeping off its revels of the night before.

"How did you know it was me?" My voice was a smooth baritone that always felt sexy sliding past my lips.

"For one thing, there aren't many people out and no one else was standing in front of the bar."

"I could have gotten someone to stand here while

I blended in over there." I gestured toward the bus shelter.

"True, but I think such a game at the start of a business meeting would be beneath you. Also," he pointed to my neck. "You have a small mark on your neck that seems to be there regardless of what form you're in."

How had he noticed that? It was the one thing I was never able to change, and I had to remember whenever I really needed to make sure I wasn't recognized to cover it with either an accessory or skin-toned tape. But it was tiny, shaped like the kind of curvy V one would use to depict a bird flying in the distance. The fact that he picked up on such a small detail told me I needed to be on my toes with this guy.

"By the way..." his eyes slowly appraised me from foot to head and back down. "You look *quite* hand-some." His voice was low and husky, only meant for my ears.

Before I recovered from being flustered at the compliment, he was holding the door to the car open.

When Dúl had mentioned going to his office in Manhattan, I somehow convinced myself we would be taking the train. Imagining staring out over the choppy waters of the Hudson, I had not expected a limousine with dark tints, a uniformed driver, and a privacy shield.

“What’s all this?” I blurted.

“I know,” Dúl said from beside the open rear door. “The Night Lanes would get us there in a matter of minutes in Waking time, but you never know what creatures you'll encounter there. Plus, this will give us a chance to talk."

I nodded and stepped into the earthiness of leather, the tang of gin, the bouquet of wine, and the lush sweetness of chocolate. Attached to the front seats was a small bar beneath the privacy shield. I slid over to make room for Dúl.

"You sprayed this baby with 'new car smell,' didn't you? Tell the truth," I said.

He grinned. "Only the best for you. It was the most expensive 'new car' spray we could find. Drink?"

I shrugged. "Sure."

"Alcohol, virgin cold, or virgin hot?" His lips twitched.

Stifling a laugh, I let my knees spread. "Cocoa."

He reached under the bar for a thermos and a bowl-sized mug. The brown liquid steamed as he poured it. It tasted sweet and rich. All this luxury was a far cry from life in the Fringe.

I leaned back in my seat and sighed. "So where exactly are we headed?"

"The Shadow Lord—"

"Seriously, doesn't he have a name like a normal person?"

"Only a select few people outside the family know it. Names have power, after all. I think you'd agree...Umbra."

Surprised as I was to hear my birth name come out of Dúl's mouth, the only sign I gave was a slight tremor of my hand holding the mug. I covered that by bringing the drink to my lips.

Once I felt composed, I responded. "I won't ask where you picked that intel up."

"The Shadow Network is extensive if slightly un-disciplined. There isn't much we don't know. *Your* information wasn't hard to come by at all."

I mentally ran through the few people who could sell me out. Rebus and Nat? Not in this lifetime. Paris? Not likely, although if he had been hard up for a fix....

My teeth clenched. I longed to ask the question, but pride won out. Dúl saved me.

"No one betrayed you, Merc. And your secret is safe with me. Rumor has it that you spent time in the Courts? Do you remember it at all?"

I watched the stores along Route 59 fly by and recalled the only time in my life I had ever been cap-tured without meaning to be.

I had been living alone on the streets...somewhere tropical. One day, I meandered into a misty rain forest. Within minutes, men in strange green armor that was shaped like giant leaves picked me up and carried me off. I couldn't fight them, so I did the next best thing: I shifted into a tiny snake and escaped.

"When I was little. I remember wandering around the Summer Court. I stayed there for a while, but I never felt comfortable there. Everyone was too...perky. Noisy. Always partying. It didn't seem right with-out my parents, even though I didn't remember what happened to them or their faces to describe them." I glanced back at Dúl. "So I left."

"Left? You evaded the armies of three courts!" Dúl's laugh sent a warmth through me that I didn't expect. "Would you ever consider going back?"

"To stay? Doubtful, but you never know. I like my freedom a little too much to pledge my firstborn child and my left arm to some monarch who just wants to use me to get at their siblings."

"I assure you, nothing so extreme goes on in the Courts. Your left arm would be useless without the rest of you." He grinned and poured himself a glass of seltzer. "Seriously, how would their 'use' of your talents differ from your current clientele? Except maybe that the rulers can actually afford you."

I thought about it. "Like you said yourself, the Courts have resources—armies and all kinds of people to defend their lands. The people I contract with have no one and nothing. They need me a lot more."

"I see. Well, I don't want to speak out of turn, but I would imagine that if you ever changed your mind, the Shadow King would probably welcome you with open arms. Ever since your escapades at the age of— what was it, six? seven?—he's had the Network keep loose tabs on your whereabouts. From a distance, of course."

"So, he's a stalker."

"Potential benefactor. Come now, Merc, are you telling me he's the only party who's been intrigued by your shapeshifting?"

I thought of Donny and frowned.

"He's been mainly occupied with fighting his brother, but only a fool would have let such a rare talent as yours fall off his radar completely. You've made more of a name for yourself over the past three or four years. He began to take a closer interest." It sounded less creepy when he put it like that, so I let the issue drop.

"The king actually has a great deal of respect for privacy. And surveillance. Both industries have proven quite profitable for the Shadow Court." He puffed his chest the slightest bit. Why was he telling me these things? Was it so important for me to have a positive view of the king and his court?

In any case, the Shadow King seemed like someone I could respect, maybe even get along with.

Dúl and I drank in silence as we sped toward the city. I wondered, for the first time, if I *could* ever see myself swearing loyalty to one of the Courts. The thought sent a shudder through me as I closed my eyes to let the car's vibrations silence my thoughts. A relentless sense of foreboding followed me into an uneasy doze.

Interlude: Donny

"Don't take your eyes off her, no matter what." One simple sentence. How hard was that to follow? In the forty years since he'd come to the Fringe from the Winter Court, the level of stupidity around him never failed to surprise him.

The inch-thick chain drooped from one hand as he inspected the lock at the end. How had Merc beaten the new security?

He ignored the guard's pleas for release. "Shut up, moron. You got yourself beat up by that dumb bitch, you can stay in there 'til you rot. The hell am I paying you clowns for?"

Focusing his attention on the lock, Donny willed the tumblers and iron shell to freeze. His hand shook with the effort as he squeezed. White tendrils spiraled from his hand.

The lock remained unharmed. And still secured. His new partners assured him that the new equipment was immune to magic. So how'd she do it?

Even armed with guns, his men couldn't stop her. The thought of her going toe to toe with the dumb brute now handcuffed to the cell bars sent a ripple of excitement through him. As much as he hated Merc, he couldn't deny the bulge growing behind the zipper of his gray Burberry slacks.

He'd seen her shapeshifting tricks, but whenever he imagined her, it was always as a young woman. He didn't much care what else she wanted to look like or call herself.

The sound of flesh pounding flesh was as clear in Donny's mind as if he were watching the brawl right now. He flexed a bicep that strained against his tailored, pale-yellow shirtsleeve, and with his free hand, he adjusted himself once in his pants. *Next time, I deliver the ass-kicking.*

He should have come sooner. These fools couldn't get anything right. Anyway, he hadn't gotten up close and personal with her in a while. Over a month. Too long. He envisioned her in the cell, wrists cuffed at the head of the bed, ankles bound to the corners at the foot of the bunk. Lower belly exposed. The thin line of tiny hairs curling against cherrywood tones of her skin. Skin that would turn crimson as it froze. The line of red disappearing beneath her panties.

He'd never explored further than that with Merc. At fifty-two years old, he'd learned that the mystery is always more satisfying than reality when it came to tricks like her. She'd tried making herself ugly or shifting into a dude, but there was no less satisfaction in hearing her pain. And he knew what she really looked like under the masks. She couldn't fool him.

With his new partnership, he'd teach her a real lesson. Knock that stuck-up bitch down a peg or two. She thought she was such hot shit because of her powers and because she had a college degree. Big fucking deal. Book smarts would only take her so far in the Fringe. She'd see that soon enough.

Tired of the guard's moaning, Don pulled a large key from his pocket and opened the cell. "Get the hell outta here." Then he settled in the rickety chair behind the desk—nowhere near as comfortable as the one in his office upstairs—and allowed his mind to wander to the past.

Merc hadn't always been so full of herself. First time he laid eyes on her, she was nothing but a scared little shit that couldn't even control the shape changes.

There she was one night, picking in the dumpster behind that other dumb fuck's bar. Donny had seen her and knew she'd be a big hit with his clientele. Whatever way they chose to use her was none of his concern. So many lucrative opportunities. With some training, she'd be able to obtain valuable intel on all his enemies, and that was just the beginning.

He'd cornered Merc at the back of the alley, her eyes going wide, first brown, then blue, then hazel. He could hear stray dogs fighting in the distance. One yelped, making the dirty little girl jump right out of her skin. Dropping to one knee, as if he were proposing, he'd fingered her hair—blond... red... gray... black—fascinated by the kaleidoscope effect of the changes that sped up along with her breath.

"You hungry, little rabbit? I got something for you. Wanna come with your old friend, Donny? Get you a nice, hot meal? Warm bed? Donny'll take good care of you."

"I'm sure you would, Don, but I've got this." Rebus. That guy never minded his fucking business. Donny had half a mind to freeze Rebus's balls and watch them fall off, but the former Winter spy's reputation was quite nasty. Not worth the fight. The Winter Queen had twisted that one's mind but good.

The kid would be alone at some time or other, and then Donny would strike.

Except, Rebus had watched her like a daddy hawk after that night. Taught her to control her changes among other interesting skills. Other *useful* skills. Donny had tried to entice her into the business in so many ways, he'd lost count. She had *even* turned into a fine piece of ass. Merc became attractive to him on a whole other level. He chuckled. *Lotta fine asses all in one.*

But she thought she was too good for him.

Of course, she did, after Rebus filled her head with so much bullshit.

Now though, Donny knew something Rebus didn't. The ace he had up his sleeve would bring Merc around. He stood, reached into his slacks, fixed his pecker again to walk more comfortably, and headed upstairs. Schemes wound through his brain.

She had messed up his plans for the last time. Now he would hurt her worse than any punch in the gut ever could. She'd beg to serve him. The final nail in that coffin would be driven home any day now.

Maybe he'd send a note like she'd done so many times to him.

There was always the chance she could be reasonable. He hoped not.

In the meantime, he stepped over the unconscious guards, went into his office, and shut the door. Maybe he'd give those two bozos to the bloodsuckers as a gift. From the middle drawer of his mahogany desk, he withdrew a Cuban cigar. The lighter hissed and clicked before releasing a small flame. As he puffed in, Donny dialed his newest recruit.

The phone rang too many times before there was an answer. They'd have to work on that.

"Hey, Boss." The sound of wind combined with the kid talking louder than usual told Donny he had to be outside.

"Took you so long? When the Don calls, you answer. Immediately. Got it?"

"Yeah, sorry about that. Needed to get someplace quiet. Everything good?"

"Nah, but we got more important things to discuss. Got another job for you. Bigger. Better compensation. You in?"

The whoosh of a vehicle zooming by. "Hell yeah. Whatchu need?"

"That's what I like to hear." Donny took a long drag and released the smoke in an expert ring. "Got some bloodsuckers need a guide again."

"Uh, sure. Daytime?"

"Heh, you wish, kid. Total pussies during the day,

right? Sadly for you, no. Nighttime. You get them in and out of where they need to go and then be on your merry way. You'll be safe enough."

"Oh, nah, Boss. I wasn't—"

"Whatever. You in?"

"Yeah, no doubt."

Donny provided the details and ended the call. Waving the cigar smoke from in front of his eyes, he smiled. *Let's see what kind of love note she sends me when she hears about this.*

Chapter 5

I must have made up for my lack of sleep because before I knew it, the George Washington Bridge was spanning the river toward New Jersey. My hands were empty. The half-full mug of cocoa sat safely on the bar. A stealthy swipe across my chin reassured me that I hadn't drooled during the hour-long ride.

Against the seat, Dúl's head lolled to the side. He appeared mostly human, the only signs of his fey-dom being points at the tips of his ears. He could pass as a goth.

A hot Goth with long...really nicely muscled legs. Look away!

Although his eyes were shut, I doubted he was asleep. To test my theory, I leaned forward toward the privacy glass.

"We should be there in about ten minutes," he said, eyes still closed.

"You didn't need to pretend sleep if you didn't want to talk."

"Resting my poor, dazzled eyes. And I didn't want

you to think I had been watching you sleep like some sort of creep."

"Um, yeah. That would be awkward."

Now that he mentioned watching me, my face heated. I straightened my glasses and looked out the window. Was he flirting? I spent so much time fighting and working, I almost forgot what that looked and sounded like. Didn't matter. I shouldn't let myself get distracted by whatever he was trying to do.

Thankfully, we soon arrived at a tall, glass building. The car pulled into an underground garage, and we got out in front of an elevator.

The elevator panel had buttons for two garage levels, thirty-five floors, a penthouse, and an unlabeled button that lit up without Dúl touching it. When the bell dinged, we stepped onto gray marble floors. A vacant reception desk stood between us and a glass wall with a huge silhouette of a black bird. Beneath the logo, a sign read, *RavCorp*. As Dúl approached it, a section of the wall swung out. He waved me through.

Gray plush carpeted the floor on this side of the glass. Pairs of black leather couches faced each other across marble and glass coffee tables. The waiting area overlooked an amazing view of the Hudson.

Dúl led me down a hall to the right. We made another turn and entered a windowless office bigger than my apartment. Blue lights supplied dim illumination. About two-thirds of the way into the room was a huge, black desk, bare and flanked by three chairs —two forward and one behind. Beyond the desk, outlines of trees rose past the point where I could see the tops. The entire wall appeared to be a dark tank.

Before I could ask, Dúl took my hand and led me over to see a forest landscape behind glass.

"Trees?"

Silently, he pointed. From a shadow perched on a branch, round, yellow eyes gazed at me. They slowly blinked.

"An owl?"

"Oedipus. He'll be going out hunting soon, I expect. An access panel allows them to come and go."

"Them?"

As the word left my mouth, two black bullet-shaped objects shot toward a little pond at the bottom of the enclosure. Two loud caws greeted us.

"Jekyll and Hyde," Dúl said. "My best messengers."

The ravens paused from drinking to look up at Dúl. He nodded, they returned the gesture, and he walked back toward his desk.

Distracted by the habitat, I had ignored the L-shaped couch and loveseat arranged around a brick fireplace on the left side of the room. The right side, near the door, had a treadmill, trampoline, massive flat screen TV, and a video game setup.

Dúl sat. I stood, gaping.

"You could fit three families from the Fringe in here. They'd be pretty freakin' comfortable."

"This disturbs you?"

He waved his hand, a tail of shadow following its arc. The air shimmered as if it had all been a mirage, and the room shrank to a fraction of its earlier size. All that remained was a plain oak desk with a chair on each side. Gray stone replaced the aviary. The temperature dropped. Goosebumps prickled my arms.

"Better?" Dúl said with a cold smile that showed a bit too much tooth enamel.

I scowled. "No. You don't have to act all offended. The other way was fine. I was just saying."

"I understand," he said. His face relaxed. "The poverty in the Fringes is unfortunate, but at least for the changelings, there is an alternative. Living under the protection of the Courts has its perks. Shall we get to work?"

With another wave of his hand, the real office returned. I sat opposite him and watched as a large world map shimmered into existence on the desktop. The upper left corner read, *The Waking*. The air quavered again, and another, transparent map floated down covering the first. Its right corner was labeled, *The Dreaming.*

"Did Rebus ever explain to you just how the Three Realms interact?"

"Yeah, sure," I said, leaning in to see the maps better. Pointing, I said, "The Dreaming is a separate plane superimposed over the Waking, and the Fringes are spots in between where portals connect the two. Only fullbloods and changelings can use the portals at will, but once in a while mortals and other mythic races, like the vamps, find their way in. The Night Lanes run through everything." I grinned. "Wanna hear my fifth-grade math text next?"

He chuckled. "No, thanks. What of the Courts?"

"Don't know too much about them. Pretty much just avoid them."

I expected him to give me one of those looks that made me feel like a poor, misguided fool for hesitating to spend the rest of my life in servitude to one of the fey royals. That was the unspoken downside of "living under the protection of the Courts" as Dúl put it. As far as I was concerned, it meant you were stuck.

The pity never came. I was a little disappointed that he didn't even glance up at me.

Dúl used his finger to pinpoint different-colored, glowing lines on the transparency. "These lines delineate the borders between the Courts."

The Winter Court controlled the territories at each of the earth's poles, while Summer occupied the area between the Tropics of Cancer and Capricorn. Between the queens' realms, the kings split the lands evenly with Dawn closer to his warm sister and Shadow near his glacial sister's home.

Dúl pointed at South Florida. "Dawn and Summer meet here."

"Hold on," I said, "New York is barely above the line between your Court and Dawn, which stretches down to Florida."

"Yes."

"Where's Morgan?" I knew I wouldn't like the answer.

He pointed. "Nassau."

"The Bahamas? Are we planning a rescue or a spring break?"

All kinds of warning bells went off in my head along with Internet headlines of girls disappearing from the Caribbean. I barely knew this guy. I couldn't go to some tropical island alone with him. Paris would have a conniption, even if I went in this body. I held my hands up in a warding-off gesture.

"Whoa. You never said anything about leaving the country. I don't even know you. Second—"

"You have nothing to fear from me. I'll be happy to take a blood oath if that will ease your mind."

Death if he broke his promise? Sounded reasonable.

"Okay, but second, how are we supposed to get through the Dawn lands? Isn't that illegal for you?"

"Yes and no. We can travel the Night Lanes into Cuba. My lord will ask his sister to allow us to move through her lands, which she will almost certainly allow. From there, you will continue to Nassau, alone. That will minimize my time in the Dawn lands. I'll meet you and Morgan at an extraction point. Precise timing is going to be key."

Doubts surfaced. Unfriendly territories were nothing new to me, but I had rarely dealt directly with full-bloods and or with their level of magic. I could handle this. Probably.

"Just to be clear, she's in the Waking, right?" Their powers were stronger in the Dreaming.

Dúl nodded. "Yes. Keeping her in the Dreaming

would be catastrophic. Orion is probably only keeping her to annoy the Shadow Lord, so probably not worth escalating hostilities to the degree that keeping her in the Dreaming would."

But what was she doing there in the first place? I'd heard enough and dropped the subject. Fey politics were none of my business. The job was.

This was bigger than anything I had ever tried. I paced between the aviary and the desk, trying to think of the ways that this could be a trap to trick me to work for the Shadow Court, or that Dúl could screw me over. Unfortunately, it could be, and he might. Still, my gut said to go for it.

"Okay. Let's do it."

Interlude: Summer and Shadow

The king materialized from a swirl of shadow and strode up the palm-lined path toward the veranda where his sister reclined in a hammock. She sipped from a straw poking out of a green coconut shell. The mocha skin of her oiled scalp gleamed as bright as her smile. She wore gauzy yellow pants with a matching bandeau top.

"Brother! To what do I owe this surprise? I've told you a million times, I'm not taking sides between you and Orion. Boring as he is, he's my big brother too."

The Summer Queen waggled her eyebrows and grinned. It was difficult for the Shadow King to see his favored sibling as an adult and not the precocious child she had once been.

"I haven't come for that, Sister. Although, after what he's done this time, you might see things differently. Morgan is missing." The king sauntered up three steps and leaned against a white column, crossing ankles and arms. Fitted gray slacks hugged his hip, and a silver silk button down was open at the top.

"Your intended finally had enough of your rejection, and now you think she's run off with Orion? Have you gone mad?" Her laugh tinkled like bells. "Who would ever be that desperate? He's no fun! Anyway, he's already bound to his consort. I'm sure Morgan will be back when she's ready." With a majestic wave of her hand, an attendant glided over, dressed exactly as Athena with an identical shaved head. "Drink? Luz can get you whatever you want."

He ignored his sister's way of envisioning the most simplistic solutions to every problem. Not everything could be fixed with a smile and a drink. She meant well. "Morgan came to me a few days ago with information that Orion had stolen my Shadow dagger. When I told her to have someone retrieve it, I did not expect her to take on the task herself. She—"

"Well, as talented as your network is, darling, you must admit, they do lack focus." The hammock swayed lazily from side to side.

The king scowled. "I'm working on that. Will you let me finish, please?"

With an expression of mock innocence, and a fake pout, Athena quieted and shrugged.

"Thank you. She never returned, so I expect he's detained her. I'd appreciate leave to send in...an independent agent... through your lands and into Orion's. Just a retrieval mission, nothing more."

His sister watched him and tapped her bottom lip with trimmed, unadorned fingernail. "I don't see that anything is obvious. Have you even asked Orion about it? How do you know someone isn't trying to stoke the flames between the two of you?"

"For one thing, dearest, those fires have blazed for years and need no outside fanning. For another, who would do such a thing? Not that I wouldn't." He laughed. Athena was one of the few people in his life who could make him smile. "But I'd need a valid reason."

Contrasting him, Athena's lips curled downward, replacing the previous, carefree expression. He knew what the next words would be.

"Who would do such a thing? Our sister! That evil, miserable, wrinkled—"

"Speaking of wrinkles, ranting is bad for the skin." And so was the blazing sun, which forced the king farther into the shade of the porch. He perched on a windowsill while his youngest sister spat more complaints about their eldest sibling.

"That hag wants the entire dreaming to bow down to her. To exist in gloom and cold like she does. Can you honestly trust that *she* didn't abduct your betrothed?"

He winced. "Please don't call her that. And no, I don't trust Nemesis in the slightest. However, I do *understand* her. Taking Morgan would gain her nothing. She didn't do it. I *know* Orion is behind this."

Athena harrumphed, and there was genuine ire behind her pout now. "Your agent may travel through my lands, of course, but I believe you are wrong about this."

"Noted, dear, and thank you. By the way, you might come visit some time. I loathe having to endure all this heat and brightness every time I wish to see you."

"Ugh. Your realm is almost as cold and depressing as the Winter Court." His sister glared at him for moment and then softened. "Perhaps during the rainy season. Try to stay out of trouble in the meantime."

He leaned down to kiss her forehead and then plunged himself into a cool, black spiral of darkness.

Chapter 6

Dúl left me alone in the office. Overdressed for a trek through the Night Lanes, I transformed. Since I didn't know what we might encounter, I wanted the form I could move in the easiest. My outfit was simplified—black combat boots, cotton tank, leather jacket, thick denim jeans. I checked my new bracelet to make sure it was secure and felt for my picks tucked into my rebraided hair.

I called Paris's cell. After the fourth ring, he slurred a greeting. Several voices murmured in the background.

An unbidden memory seized my mind—Paris at the back of an alley with several vampire women latched onto his various veins. He was barely conscious, not because of the blood loss, but because he had nearly overdosed. For a month afterward, every day was a fight as I tried to force him to give up the drugs cold turkey. We barely left the apartment. I thought I could cure him.

I still don't know how I managed to earn a four-year degree. With all the shit Paris and I went through, that was nothing short of a miracle.

The day he ventured back out alone for the first time, I followed him. He went straight to his dealer and made a buy.

After that, I gave him an ultimatum. Since I couldn't manage it, he had to go into rehab. A few three-month stints later, and here we were again.

I tried to swallow my annoyance. "Hey, babe. I'll be away for a couple of days. Work. Just wanted to check in."

"Paying work or another charity job? What time is it, anyway?"

Was he kidding? "The better question is: where are you? And where were you all day?"

"Fuck, Merc. You wake me up to fight? I crashed with some friends. Chill."

"Friends. Do these *friends* have tits and fangs?"

As soon as I said it, as if responding to the accusation, a female giggled. She was too close to his phone.

"Bastard," I told Paris. "Who's not keeping up their end of the deal now? You promised to stay clean and stay away from those bloodsucking bitches." My voice remained quiet and composed, but if I gripped my phone any harder, it would crumble.

"I'm not high! I was sleeping. Fucking relax."

"Relax?" This call was a mistake. I couldn't do this with him now—I needed to focus. "I'll relax. Have fun."

I jabbed the END button.

After I had taken several deep breaths, sniffled a couple of times, and paced a few laps around the office, Dúl reemerged. He had changed into more practical attire as well—jeans, a T-shirt, and heavy boots. Stopping in front of me, he cocked his head and scowled. "Is there some problem? You seem unsettled."

I coughed to clear my throat. "Nope. All good."

It seemed he wanted to say more but didn't. He held his hand out to me.

"You know how to do this?"

I curled my lip and glared. He couldn't be serious. The question was practically a professional insult.

He nodded and clasped my hands. We both closed our eyes to enter a trance state.

The Night Lanes are made of nightmares. The traveler's fears form their landscape. Imagining monsters jumping from around corners will produce those monsters. The trick to moving through them safely is to control those fears.

Using the Lanes alone is safer but more difficult in the same way that building a tower of blocks is slower when doing it on your own. Yet the more people who travel together, the more opportunities for nasty stray thoughts to cause problems. I suspected Dúl could control his fears well.

It's also necessary to know how to navigate the Lanes. I stink at it. When I've had to use them in an escape, I've winged it, ended up somewhere weird, and traveled back to safety through the Waking.

When I opened my eyes, we were on a cobblestone street. Iron gas lamps burned at regular intervals. A thin layer of fog rolled over the ground. In the distance, I heard an occasional whooping laugh, or the click-clack of horse hooves. A pissy odor filled my nostrils.

This scene of my recurring nightmare was all too familiar. The idea of Jack the Ripper always scared me. What if he had never been caught because he had wandered into the Dreaming? Stranger things have happened. I could manage this.

I picked a line of stones to focus on and tried to keep my mind clear. Dúl linked his fingers with mine and squeezed. We started down the street.

"So," he said with a light tone. "Tell me why you avoid the Courts."

I appreciated the distraction. "Tell me why anyone would want to be stuck in one place forever."

He laughed. "What makes you think that? The Courts are huge—you saw that from the map. Fey move in and out of the Dreaming all the time. There are multiple options. Plus, each Court is *really* only banned from one of the other three."

"Didn't know that."

A cat yowled. Something crashed. I forced myself not to look.

"You know how to navigate this place, right?" My voice was as light as his had been.

"At least as well as you do."

I glanced over to see a crooked smile. I had to chuckle. My hand felt warm in his. Some of the ground fog cleared.

"So, what's your Court like? All I remember was that it was cold."

Whispers behind me. A shadow crossed my peripheral vision then disappeared. I watched the cobblestones as we walked past them.

"Sometimes it is," Dúl said. "The weather varies. But it's always dusk. No bright sunrises. The sky is always filled with the deep oranges, pinks, and purples of sunset."

Dúl's head turned sharply to the left, then forward. "Let's turn down this street."

It had no lamps. The light from the main road only reached in a few feet. My heartbeat quickened. I closed my eyes, trying to maintain control.

"Trust me, Merc. We're fine. Tell me about your boyfriend. That ought to be a pleasant topic. You live together, right?"

He couldn't have known that would be a sore subject. Most girls in their early twenties—changeling, fey, or human—love to talk about boyfriends. Since I wore this female body more often than any other, it was reasonable for him to assume I identified and behaved as what he saw. But I had never fit the patterns of 'most' *anything,* certainly not most girls. I've always been a touch different and just *me*—literally an embodiment of anything and everything.

When I thought of Paris now, I remembered the giggling in the background. I remembered how cold his side of the bed had been while I was failing to sleep earlier. I remembered how he had grabbed my arm last night.

A body barreled into me from behind. My hand

slipped from Dúl's. I found myself alone in the dark alley, my face smashing into the ground. A heavy male figure pinned me. From each side, hissing female voices taunted me. Heavy breaths steamed into my ear as a cold metal blade kissed my throat.

"Get off my back, Merc. Get it? Back?" The sinister laugh sounded like a monstrous version of Paris's. "Just relax now. This won't be quick." I knew it wasn't him but froze. The blade against my skin heightened the pain of the last words he had said to me. "Fucking relax." It was valid advice.

He wouldn't hurt you. Not like this. It's not real.

But a wound *would* be real. If I died here, that would be real, too.

While I convinced myself to get up and fight, Dúl cursed and shouted my name. "Merc! Where are you?"

Paralyzed, my voice wouldn't come. The blade at my throat could slice skin the moment I uttered a sound. The thing on my back compressed my lungs, and its knife pressing harder against my windpipe. I squeezed my eyes shut. *Relax. Focus.*

Finally, my brain kicked into gear. The monster couldn't slit my throat if there wasn't a throat to slit. I concentrated on the form I intended to take. My body lengthened, stretched, the bones and vertebrae melting into scales and muscle. The transformation was almost instantaneous, much faster than if I were in the Waking. A moment later, I coiled around my attacker's throat and hissed. Then my venomous fangs tore into his neck. With a small pop, he disappeared.

"Merc? Merc! Answer me, damn it!"

As a giant cobra, I didn't need to see Dúl to find him. The vibrations of his boots scuffing against the stone led me to him, as he moved in a small circle of complete darkness. I flicked out my tongue and savored the differences in the air. He tasted of earth and warm spices and apples. I slithered over toward him and shifted back. "Here. I'm here."

Once I was standing before him, he grabbed my hand, and we rushed out of the alley toward another street with lights. The voices of the Paris monster and his groupies followed us, whispering on the night breeze.

In the lit area, Dúl stopped abruptly to check me over. "Are you alright? I couldn't see anything. I just heard women saying...never mind. I'm sorry. I hadn't realized it would be a dangerous conversation starter."

I let him ramble. Why did he seem so freaked out? We hadn't gone through with the blood oath about my safety. This guy had so many sides. For some strange reason, his quirks calmed me.

"I'm fine. Really. Let's move."

"Right." He smiled. "Merc, AKA 'Fine.' I'm sorry that happened. I can do amazing things with shadows—"

"If you do say so yourself." I said, teasing, but he didn't take the bait.

"—but with no light...I should have had you carry a flashlight or something. Once your...weakness was triggered, my fear kicked in. I wasn't thinking ...distracted..."

"It's okay. Seriously. Let's just get out of here."

The voices were coming back, and unless my eyes were tricking me, the lamps seemed dimmer. I took his hand. We jogged.

Running drowned out the voices. Dúl and I fell into a rhythm together. After ten minutes, the landscape brightened. And continued to brighten. Too much.

We were in a vast desert. The sun scorched us in our dark clothing. *This must be one of his fears.* Of course, a wide-open, bright space would make a Shadow fey uncomfortable. The heat forced us to slow to a walk.

It was my turn to put Dúl's mind on something else. "Are we close? I don't think I've ever been to Cuba. Or the Bahamas for that matter, but I could be wrong."

He glanced at me with an arched eyebrow. "You don't know because you don't remember your child-hood?"

"Yeah. No idea where I'm from except that it's somewhere near the Summer Court."

"So, it's possible you're from Cuba."

"Yes, but not likely. I'm pretty sure I never crossed any bodies of water, and the Night Lanes would've been traumatic. I figure I must have been somewhere in Central or South America."

He paused, as if digesting my theory. "Would you like to find out some day?"

"Maybe? But I may not like what I find if I go digging, so..."

"So, let's change the subject."

We trudged along for a while longer. The level of

comfort I felt with Dúl surprised me. That kept me calm as we continued across the sand to a beach.

"Speaking of crossing water..." I said. "Can you swim?"

His eyes sparkled with mischief. "Can you?"

"Nope. But I can turn into a big-ass fish." I grinned.

This had to be the strangest trip through the Night Lanes in history. Were we actually making jokes?

"Okay, tell you what. You turn into a...dolphin. I'll ride on your back."

"I may charge you extra for taxi service."

"Put it on my tab."

Once I waded into the water, I transformed. This was a new form for me, but I didn't want to let on, so I wracked my brains for anything I had learned about dolphins in school. *No gills, lungs. How long can I stay under before I have to come up for air? Shit.* I tested my tail. Weird that it worked vertically instead of horizontally, but it felt natural. The water lapping along my sides was soothing. The form would take over. They always did.

Dúl followed, fully dressed, and moved to my side. Then he darkened and dissolved until the water where he had been looked like a shadow played over it. I felt his hand on my dorsal fin, but when I started swimming, he was weightless.

The speed was incredible, like torpedoing through a time warp.

Shortly, we approached the Bahama Islands.

I spared a split second's thought: *Thank goodness, nothing stopped us.*

Jinxed it.

A huge shark with gigantic teeth bubbled into existence about a hundred yards in front of us. I may have had the body of a dolphin, but the brain was still all me. I tried to flip and swim away.

Dúl's voice echoed in my head. "Easy, Merc. Just keep moving forward. He won't see you. Trust me."

Putting my faith in him, I did as Dúl said. The water around me dimmed, as if night had fallen.

The shark veered left at the last second.

We made it to the island with no further problems. Dúl was as dry as he had been when we were in the desert. Clasping hands, we shut our eyes.

"*Yumé,*" we said together. When we opened them, we were in the Dreaming—in the Summerlands.

Chapter 7

As if it had been a matter of days since I had been there instead of years, I at once recognized the Summerlands. The weather was steamy and hot. A citrusy aroma permeated the air, and everything sparkled like every surface was crusted with diamonds in sunlight. The whole place was killing my eyes.

I blinked several times and then threw my arms around Dúl's neck. "How did you do that? With the shark? I thought we were chum!"

He hugged me back, a little longer than expected. I didn't complain.

"I told you, I'm amazing with shadows. You're not the only one who can take a different form." He winked. "Although I've never seen another changeling do what you can."

"I'm one of a kind."

"One of a kind you are." He tugged a braid. Our eyes locked.

I noted that his other hand still rested on my left hip, and my hands still lounged on his biceps. What the hell was I doing?

I suddenly had to get out of that leather jacket. Reluctantly, I pulled away.

"So, um...do I leave from here or cross into the Waking?"

Dúl cleared his throat and ran a hand through his hair. "Waking. I'll escort you to a private yacht that will take you to the marina in Nassau. You'll remember the rest of the instructions from there?"

"You'll remember to be at the extraction point tomorrow night?"

He grinned. "Touché."

~*~

Dúl had arranged to have an array of outfits available on the yacht for me. My heartstring tugged a bit when I registered men's, women's, and genderless options in more sizes than I could imagine. I settled on a turquoise bikini top with flowy, wide-leg pants to match. I decided that a shorter, curvy body type would serve me well once on the island. My hair flew wild and kinky, just the way I liked it, except for two thin braids just big enough to fit my picks, held back by a seashell clip.

My skin tingled as it darkened several shades. The wound on my shoulder had mostly disappeared, the skin of the scar only the slightest bit shinier. Stretching and molding, my face became rounder with fuller lips. I checked the mirror and lightened my eyes to a nice shade of hazel, even though I wore oversized sunglasses.

All that took about fifteen minutes. Another five

went toward finding places to conceal as many of my tools as I could. My wrist cuff looked good with the outfit. I strapped daggers to my thighs and ankles above Roman-style sandals. No matter how hard I tried, I couldn't avoid carrying a purse.

Once disguised, I spent the next forty minutes rehearsing the plan, or at least trying to. My brain made many side treks: What had the vamp women said to Dúl in the Night Lanes? Was I losing Paris to his habits again? Other thoughts interrupted about Dúl's relationship with Morgan.

I jammed all the distractions into a mental lockbox and refocused on the job. As soon as I left the cabin, I ran right into him.

"You look enchanting." He studied me as if trying to find traces of the two other forms he'd seen that day. "I'm curious. How do you decide on your features? Is it just what moves you in the moment, or is there also an element of function? I hope that's not too rude." He had also changed again into what appeared to be a black silk tunic to his thighs and loose lounge pants of the same fabric. And he was barefoot.

"I usually end up just going with whatever is useful for the job, or if I'm not on a job, I stick to the version my boyfriend likes. Most of the time I don't mind, but some days..." I shrugged. I wasn't about to tell a total stranger that some days it irked me that I catered to Paris's whims when it came to my body, but he wasn't that accommodating when it came to my wants.

Dúl cocked his head to one side like he was trying

to see me from a different angle. I was surprised to not feel any need to squirm or hide. "At the risk of overstepping, it sounds like he's someone who isn't very secure in himself if he has to control your appearance."

That made me feel exposed, so I crossed my arms over my chest. "I guess I understand it—not wanting me to be in a male body if he's attracted to women."

"Are all humans so shallow? I confess there are plenty of fey who are just as... rigid." The way his fingers curled in like claws and his shoulders tightened made me wonder if he was thinking about his brother. What a pair we made!

Dúl continued, "For the record, you're quite fetching in each of the forms I've seen. But your boyfriend isn't here, so what made you choose this version of yourself?"

My cheeks heated. "Well, in this particular form, a little softer, what some would consider chubby, showing a lot of skin, people will tend to underestimate me and treat me a certain way. Men will undoubtedly flirt. Women will assume they're smarter than me. Their preconceptions can work in my favor."

"Brilliant. What a gift you have." After wishing me luck, he waved me forward, and we went up onto the deck.

Later, the water below was the clearest blue I had ever seen. All around, people meandered near swanky hotels and resorts. Despite the skimpy top that barely covered my enlarged assets, I ignored a lurch in my gut as the gangplank lowered to allow me ashore.

Off the boat, I worked my way to the next block and searched for a jitney. When I left the bus, I walked down a little hill toward a hole-in-the-wall motel called The Nassau, located on a dead-end road. Paint peeled around the doors. Some of the tiles along the walkway had chipped. Otherwise, it seemed clean enough and smelled of sea and coconut.

I found myself enjoying the way the sun blazed against my skin. It felt familiar.

When I entered the building, a medium height man with close-cropped hair stood behind the reception desk to my left. A loose, short-sleeved shirt did little to hide the belly protruding beneath it.

His brown lips spread into a wide grin. "'Ello, dahling. What can I do for you today?"

At the last second, it occurred to me that I shouldn't sound like myself.

"Hey," I drawled in my best attempt at a southern accent. "I been stayin' over at the Paradise? But I cain't stay there no more. Ya have anything available? Everyplace else seems to be full up."

I slid my glasses to the top of my head and gave the clerk my best damsel-in-distress, wide-eyed gaze. He nodded sympathetically as he ogled my bikini top. My smile remained glued in place.

"Where you from, dahling?" His eyes slowly found their way to my face.

I wiggled my butt in a quick twerk. "The ATL, baby!

Heeey!" I had no idea if girls from Atlanta behaved or spoke this way. My only point of reference was reality TV.

This was my first time out of the tri-state area since I was a kid. The lack of worldliness now seemed to be a huge gap in my professional education. I definitely needed to add traveling to my to-do list.

Whether my impersonation was right or not, the clerk's grin stretched. "Ah. Dey do good work in Atlanta. We have only one single, dahling. Dat okay?"

I rolled my weight from one hip to the other. "I'll take it." *Creep.* If this place had seen a customer in the past year, I'd chew off my left pinkie. "That's fine. My...friend will be staying right where he is."

The clerk chuckled. "Enjoying too many Bahama Mamas?"

"Mmm hmm." I nodded, snaking my neck slowly, locking eyes with this jerk's. Let him think I was vulnerable and out for revenge all he wanted.

He handed me a key card. "No luggage?"

"I'll send for it later. Right now, I need to rest."

I passed a bar tended by a dark-skinned, middle-aged woman. A younger woman with golden skin, corn-rows, and a housekeeping uniform whispered with the bartender. The maid's skin seemed pale for someone working in a tropical climate. It was hard to tell from a distance, but were her ears pointed beneath those braids? If she was fey, that meant my information was good and Morgan must be close, maybe in the hotel.

Each room on my side of the hall had a back

poolside entrance. For the rest of the day, I basked and baked, waiting for dusk, one eye always open behind my shades.

The shadows shifted. A quiet caw came from my right. I turned to see a black shape nestled behind a coconut in a palm tree. With a stretch and a yawn, I got up, returned to my room, and cracked the sliding glass door open. One of Dúl's ravens hopped in a minute later, a note clamped in its beak.

"Damn it. Why can't things ever go smoothly?" I spoke to the bird as if it could understand or respond. The note said Morgan was not in the Waking and I should continue through the portal to the Dreaming. I scribbled a quick reply to Dúl. The raven snapped up my folded note and flew out.

Two long hours of mind-numbing channel surfing passed. Finally, someone knocked. I opened the door to find Creepy Clerk leaning against the doorjamb, a large suitcase next to him.

"Taxi dropped this for your room number. Yours?"

I nodded and reached for the handle. He blocked me. "What fool boy let go such a fine woman? You deserve a man, dahling."

What fool man would leave himself so wide open to a kick in the sac? Forcing non-violent thoughts into my mind, I shouldered past him to pull the suitcase into my room.

"Thank you so much," I said, "but right now I just need to be alone." My breath hitched for effect.

I slammed the door and locked it without waiting for a response.

The suitcase held my clothes, boots, tools, and a stretchy belt pack that Rebus had made for me, which fit over my shoulder and across my back, melding to any form.

I changed into fitted black clothes and shrank my body to a more nimble, petite frame. A small nose and thin lips provided less surface area to injure if I had to fight. My skin was now as black as my gear, and my hair was pulled back into a single French braid. I could have been one of Dúl's Shadow warriors, if such a thing even existed. Petite as I was, I felt powerful. The last thing I did was slap my new cuff on my wrist before peeking through the curtain covering the sliders.

Full dark had fallen. A lovely quarter moon hung low in the sky. I crept outside, pressing close to the wall. My room was at the back of the motel, while the entrance to the Dreaming was on the sea-facing west side.

A dozen steps brought me past the pool to the corner of the building. I peeked around it. All clear. About ten yards ahead, thick mist writhed and swirled through a copse of banyan trees. I moved toward them.

Three steps. I had made it three measly steps when a door burst open. The housekeeper I had passed earlier was laughing and backing out of a room, a wine bottle in one hand. Creepy Clerk was inside, his gut poking between the hem of a tank undershirt and the waistband of plaid boxers.

I might as well have been on a stage in the center spotlight.

His mouth formed an O when he saw me. The maid stopped cackling and turned. I bounded into the trees leaving their shocked questions half uttered.

If they had any connection whatsoever to the Dawn Court, I was beyond screwed. Couldn't worry about it now. I entered the mist. Dúl would be at the extraction point soon.

In the Dawn lands, orange, pink, and gray striated the sky as the sun broke through fog. Dewdrops covered everything as if a psychotic, bedazzling rogue fey had gone berserk. My skin tingled as I paused to re-camouflage myself in paler earth tones.

The motel was gone. Behind me instead, a white sand beach sparkled toward a calm sea. Ahead, a forest of banyans stood between me and a small, lonely building about a hundred yards away. I snuck forward and listened intently for any movement around me. A shriek from above made me jump. Just an animal. At least, I convinced myself it was.

Dúl had shown me a picture of Morgan: olive skin, black bob haircut, square jaw, thick brows drawn down into a V.

When I reached the single-story building, I peeked in through a window. Inside the room was a huge bed with banyan wood growing out of the floor to create the legs and posts of its frame. The bed was neat and looked as if it had never been disturbed. I had to go in.

I scanned the area around this side of the building. The hairs along the back of my neck stood. I couldn't see any signs of surveillance. The Dawn King wouldn't leave her unguarded. Only a newb would fall for such an obvious trap. But where was it? Where was she?

Rebus taught me to look for little things that seemed out of place: an off-color flower or a tree knot that might be too smooth around the edges.

I softened my gaze, taking in the larger scope of my surroundings. Twenty feet from the building, mangoes hung from tall trees with pointy leaves. Bushes sprouted yellow elder flowers. Diagonal to my position, different shrubs had huge, palm-like leaves and flowers that resembled rosy pinecones. Those caught my attention. An electric hum seemed to come from their direction. Most of them were uniform. Except for three bright red ones. Another couple of steps, and I would have triggered the trap.

If Rebus knew the gamble I was about to take, he'd never let me hear the end of it. With a mental prayer, I brought my wrist to my lips and whispered, "*Dekrar.*"

The clear crystal on the face of the cuff shone dazzling white. One by one, three clones of me stuttered into being, like holograms. Each ran in a different direction. I stayed perfectly still, hoping I was right. I held my breath.

The first clone ran alongside the building, deeper into the woods. A flower shot after it and passed through it. The wall dissolved into water where the flower exploded. The ground trembled beneath my feet. A second clone headed toward the beach. Its flower crashed into a tree trunk. The tree melted into a puddle. The last ran at the bush. The final flower followed this version of me.

It zigged toward my hiding spot. I squeezed my eyes shut. The buzz moved away. It had looped back and blasted the bush, raining droplets down on my head.

Not my most subtle entrance, and now, I was soaked. Everything fell silent.

I waited for any other movement or sound, picked up a stone, and tossed it. *Nada.* When I felt confident no more missiles would come, I checked inside the room again.

There had been so much noise already, I had no need to be stealthy now. Withdrawing a simple rescue knife from my belt, I readied the glass punch and shifted back to my ninja image. Gripping the tool in my fist, I swung it sidearm as hard as I could. The glass shattered and crashed into the room. A siren blared. I had to find Morgan. We had minutes to get out. Maybe.

I brushed away the remaining glass using the knife handle, vaulted through the opening, and rushed in. A thick layer of dust coated the bed. No one had been here in a long time. I crossed the room to the door. Locked.

Orion's protections were probably against magic

and fullbloods. Would he have thought of mundane safeguards too? I hoped not.

I felt inside my braid for the two picks hidden in it. Once the lock was popped, the door opened into a narrow corridor with glass doors at the ends to my left and right. This was a dead end, and the outside of the building was an illusion. Morgan was not—and had not been—here.

From outside the glass doors, stomping and shouting told me I needed to move. Now.

I hustled out the window and raced toward the misty area within the trees. Behind me, the air near the building suddenly wavered as if I were seeing a mirage.

There were the guards, and they were right on my ass.

As I barreled through the portal, no one blocked me. I should have wondered about that.

Creepy Clerk and three Dawn changelings waited for me on the other side.

Chapter 8

In the moonlight, the maid from the hotel stood to the clerk's right while the other two changelings stood on his left. The fair-skinned young woman with blond cornrows in her hair held a scourge whip with a short grip and several glowing blue strips that rippled on their own.

With no time to shift forms fully, while I ran, I willed my muscles and bones to expand. Then I rushed the line, as I'd seen in so many football games, hoping to barrel between Creepy Clerk and the maid. It wasn't enough. I hadn't gained enough size to send anyone flying, but I barely managed to squeeze through.

As I passed, scourge girl slashed at me. The watery strips of the weapon caught my left forearm when I tried to protect my face. From each point of contact, stinging and numbness spread through my arm. These were no changelings, and if the fullbloods' magic was this powerful in the Waking, I was way outclassed.

She flashed a grin and charged toward me. At the last second before we collided, I ducked under her outstretched arms and used her momentum to flip her into the trees. I mentally thanked Rebus for making me take all those Aikido lessons as a kid.

A hand grabbed my shoulder. It spun me around. Without thinking, I leaned left. A fist shot past my right cheek. With my right foot, I hooked Creepy behind the knee. He faceplanted with a grunt.

I glanced at the remaining two fey. The third one with light brown skin, rippling muscles, and waist-length locs was gorgeous until he reached behind him and drew a machete that shimmered the same blue as his companion's scourge. He grinned maliciously.

My left arm was useless now, but I rushed him any-way. Once I was in close, I jammed my right fingers into his sternum, then into his windpipe. He dropped to his knees, gasping. Two kicks to the head knocked him unconscious.

The numbness spread, and my neck began to tingle. I pivoted to see the last guard, a huge, pale guy reach-ing for me with his bare hands. As I took a step in his direction, a sharp pain shot through my scalp. Creepy had one hand wrapped in my braid as his other arm locked around my waist. I was yanked backward as he pressed against me. I remembered Dúl's words about my hair. *Damn.*

The clerk whispered in my ear, "The poison will paralyze you slowly, and then you will pay the Dawn Lord a little visit, eh dahling?"

Not today. Most of my body still worked.

A small dagger was tucked into a hidden sheath in my waistband.

I stabbed Creepy Clerk in the thigh. He howled and released me.

I sliced at his face, kicked the pervy bastard in the balls, and ran toward my rendezvous point.

Before I rounded the corner of the motel, six more Dawn soldiers ran from the mists. They chased me through back streets and alleys, behind clubs and around casinos. Spells flew at me, showering me with mist when they came too close. One just missed me as I leaped over a low stone wall. Half a second after I cleared it, the wall dissolved to water.

I hated these guys.

Prickling, which I dreaded more than I did the soldiers, spread along my left side down toward my hip. With my left eye already shut and my arm out of commission, I prayed the numbness wouldn't reach my leg before I reached Dúl and safety.

I was panting now but hauled myself into an alley behind a dumpster. Reaching down to my ankle for another of my daggers, I prepared to make a last stand.

The soldiers' footsteps amplified as they approached my hiding place. I itched to shift, but with no feeling in a third of my body, that wasn't happening. My thigh had lost sensation.

One hulking fey guard rounded the corner, and I crouched into a fighting stance. Just as I was about to let my dagger fly at his throat, a smaller guard burst from behind the larger one and blew a dart at me. Before I could be embarrassed at being caught, everything went black.

I woke to painful, hot pins and needles traveling through my left side. When I moved to find a more comfortable position, the surface beneath me undulated. My stomach churned. When I opened my eyes, I froze.

A rainbow of fish surrounded and watched me as if I were in a giant fishbowl. *Not a fishbowl. Under water!*

Aquamarine liquid, bright orange corals, and waving anemones stretched in every direction as far as my eyes could see. The undulating surface beneath me took the phrase "waterbed" to a weird level. It was a smaller version of the large bubble encasing me.

As I turned my head, my eyes widened. Reclining on another bubble across from me, a huge, bare-chested, blond surfer dude tapped his finger against an electric blue sword on his lap. A necklace of shells rested against beautiful bronze pecs.

If this was a dream, I was in no rush to wake up. The Adonis stood. His board shorts rode low on his hips. He sauntered to stand in front of me and pointed the tip of the sword downward. At least he wasn't skewering me without any preliminary conversation. Randomly, I wondered if his voice would be as sexy as he was.

It didn't disappoint, although his words nearly made me groan out loud. "Good afternoon. The antidote appears to be working. Now that you are awake, perhaps you can explain to me why a shifter would be poking around my realm."

Shit. "You...you're..."

"Orion, Lord of the Dawn Court. And you are?"

"Holy shit."

He cocked a blond eyebrow.

Shock and confusion addled my brain. "I-if this is the Dawn Court, why are we underwater?" Because there weren't more pressing questions I should have asked in that moment.

Apparently fey kings were as unaccustomed to fielding dumb questions as I was to asking them. To his credit, he recovered his composure much faster than I did. "I find it most efficient to imprison criminals and spies where the prospect of drowning and decompression sickness can thwart any escape attempts."

"So that's why Morgan wasn't topside."

"Morgan? I see now. My fool brother sent you." He rubbed the space between his eyebrows, closed his eyes, and shook his head slowly. "My sister mentioned that his lieutenant had gone missing. Unfortunately for you, I don't have her. He's wasted your time and mine."

Fizz erupted from the membrane of my prison and engulfed him. A second later, the Dawn King was gone, and for the first time, I couldn't imagine a way to escape.

Interlude: Dawn and Shadow

On the waterfront of Baltimore Harbor, the Shadow King lurked in the dark recesses of a private meeting room at the border between the Shadow and Dawn courts. A splash sounded outside the door of the building that, to humans, appeared to be a fishing shack. A moment later, his most hated rival—his brother—strode in dressed in black fatigues and armed to the teeth.

Am I supposed to be intimidated? "Hardly sporting of you to shoot an unarmed monarch. Doesn't that go against your *honor*?" The last word was drawled out on a mocking whine.

"As if I'd ever trust you to come unarmed as we agreed. While I'd love to sit here bantering with you, *little* brother, let's get down to business."

Perhaps his ponytailed, annoying older sibling wasn't a complete idiot after all. The king released his hold on the dagger he'd been palming and stepped out of the dim corner, dismissing the shadows that had shielded him. "Fine. The less time in your presence, the better, *old* boy. Where are they?"

"As I said in my message, I have no knowledge of

Morgan's whereabouts, and the shifter is safe so long as she doesn't attempt to escape."

The king had a protective impulse to correct his brother's language, but an explanation would extend his time in his brother's presence, so he let the term stand. And anyway, if education was ever needed, that would be Merc's decision.

Orion continued, "I believe there is a larger question, however. Someone is obviously trying to set us even more against each other, and I think we need to put aside our differences to figure out who might gain from increased dissent among our family."

"So you're saying you didn't steal my dagger either?"

"Do you ever think? What would I possibly do with it?" With a huff, Orion moved to a wooden picnic table near the right wall of the room. A platter of fruits and a pitcher of beer had been laid out. He sat and poured himself a pint.

"You don't usually need a reason to irritate me." The Shadow Lord sat across from his brother and plucked several grapes from a small vine. "What makes you think someone is attacking our family? Athena is of a similar mind, but she thinks Nemesis is behind it all."

"She always suspects Nemesis. When the world ends, she'll find a way to blame Nemesis." Dawn sipped and then licked away the froth from his top lip. "Two of my people have also disappeared as of late."

The king couldn't hide his surprise.

"Your Shadow Network didn't inform you?"

That smug simper would look so much better wearing a boot heel.

"Morgan runs my court day-to-day, and if anyone knew of fullbloods being targeted..." They stared at each other as the beginnings of realization struck. "Who was taken from your court?" the king asked, a chill of dread creeping down his spine.

"Two of my personal guard. It's time—"

"Yes, fine. Ceasefire."

"You're the spy master—"

"I'll need my employee back. If anyone can sniff out this threat, Merc can."

"She'll be returned to your office in the Waking as good as new." Orion paused and leveled the king with a look that made him want to squirm. "If it makes you feel any better, she didn't go down easily."

"I never thought *they* did."

"Is the shifter the reason you can't forgive me for insisting that Father split the Dreaming between the four of us instead of accepting a single monarchy?"

The king started at his brother incredulously, remembering his anger the day Father informed him he'd have only a portion of the kingdom over which to reign. What a grand gesture! An honor! Father thought he'd be overjoyed. He might have swallowed the responsibility more easily if it hadn't come with a prearranged marriage as a condition.

"No brother. I hated you long before I ever laid eyes on Merc."

Chapter 9

Dressed in combat gear, Orion returned and told me I was going home. Then I blanked out again.

When I woke, a dark, leather couch creaked beneath me, and a crocheted afghan covered me. With a sigh, I snuggled into its softness. My eyelids parted to slits. I blinked a few times.

Dúl rushed into the room almost as soon as I opened my eyes. "Merc! I heard what happened. Did they harm you in any way? If they did—" He kneeled at my side and cradled my face in his hands. He must have come from a meeting because he had on a tailored charcoal suit. His tie was loosened, and the top button of his pale grey shirt was undone.

The room was small and cozy. The track lights were dimmed, yet heat radiated from them while accenting paintings and enlarged photos of ravens on the walls. A lamp on the otherwise clear desk cast a yellow aura over it.

Prone, I shifted toward the back of the sofa far enough that Dúl could perch on the edge of the cushion in front of me. "I'm okay. A little freaked out that the Dawn King felt the need to interrogate me personally, but I'm fine. He even gave me something to heal the scrapes and bruises I got fighting his guards. Those assholes were pretty awesome though to be honest."

I stopped rambling. The look in his eyes was as hard as obsidian. But when I blinked, they seemed normal again. He brushed my hair back from my forehead. Confused, I started to ask what I had missed, but he smiled crookedly as he interrupted.

"It seems our intelligence about Morgan's movements was false."

"Yeah." I sat up. The room wobbled, toppling me into Dúl's arms. "I guess the poison isn't completely out of my system yet." Our eyes locked, making me wish I could read what was behind his—what fueled the inner workings of his mind.

Once I gained equilibrium, I tucked my feet under me and let go, reluctantly, with a weak laugh. "Anyway, yeah, Orion was thrown off when I mentioned Morgan. Didn't seem like he was faking."

"No. The Dawn King is generally an up-front type. He's got all the guile of a robot."

His tone had more of a bite to it than usual, but I let the comment go. "Sounds like someone set it up hoping to make things between the two courts worse."

He huffed at that and got up to pace the room. "All four courts. The Summer Queen has accused her sister of being behind it."

"Oh-kay. Well, who else would benefit from all the

courts distracted by infighting? And would that even be the goal? I mean, one fullblood's disappearance is hardly—"

"Three."

I gaped, unable to finish my sentence. A knot of tension began to form at the base of my skull.

"Two from the Dawn Court. And it seems they thought the Shadow fey had a hand in both those disappearances until you showed up there."

An idea popped into my head, one that made little sense but felt right all the same. Even if it didn't turn out to be anything, it might be a starting point.

"Hey, remember the kid I freed the other night?"

Dúl nodded. He rejoined me on the couch and leaned in, all focus on me. His intensity stole my breath. Meanwhile, scents of autumn—apples and warm spice—filled every pore, captivating me.

"Um… you probably know I've been taking jobs like that for over a year now. Vampires snatching change-ling kids, using their blood to synthesize the 'it' party drug. Lately, I've noticed that the traffic has slowed down to almost nothing."

"What do you make of that?"

"Well, it could mean nothing. Or it could mean that changeling blood isn't strong enough."

He seemed to consider my words. "Even if that were true, how would they get into the Dreaming? Only fullbloods and changelings can find the portals or use the Night Lanes."

"Unless they have a guide. Like maybe a changeling who makes their money off trafficking."

"Hmm..." Dúl's expression revealed nothing about what he was thinking. Finally, he said, "If that were true, I'd say that changeling might have a very short life expectancy."

Still slightly dizzy but energized at the prospect of a lead, I swung my feet to the floor. "I can ask Rebus what he's seen or heard and then hunt around, maybe stake out Donny's—"

"You can't be serious. You can barely sit upright, Merc. Why don't you rest—"

"No way. You're paying me to get Morgan back, so until I do, I'm still on the clock."

He frowned, skeptical, but I was pumped. If it turned out Donny had something to do with this, nothing would make me happier than to bring him down. Nothing except a fat paycheck in my pocket as I watched the fey tear him to pieces.

It was the middle of the day by the time I dragged my aching body home. Emptiness greeted me like a slap to the face. Sadly, Paris's continued absence wasn't a surprise.

A hot shower and a shift of forms helped my physical body but did nothing to improve my agitation with my missing man. Maybe to irritate him if he turned up, I chose my male form, jeans, combat boots, and a leather jacket over a black tee. When I was dressed,

I stifled the reflex to go looking for Paris and went straight to Rebus's instead.

Using my key to enter the apartment, I found him at a small dining table surrounded by metal and gears. A strap around his head attached a loupe to one eye, making his halo of hair poke up in crazy directions. This mad-scientist look always brought a smile to my face.

When Rebus noticed me approaching behind him, he jumped up, dropped the tiny grey object he had been holding, and pushed the eyepiece to the crown of his head. "Merc!" His arms crushed me to him in a warm hug. "How'd it go? Everything okay?"

I tried not to wince. "Interesting question. I got my ass handed to me by some Dawn soldiers. Safe to say, that's one court you'll never see me joining. Jerks."

My grumbling made him arch an eyebrow and frown.

"I'm fine. My ego took the biggest hit. And there's been a complication. Got a minute?"

"Of course. Nat's out shopping, but I think we got some chips..." He bustled into the kitchen and searched the upper cabinets.

Leaning against the sink opposite where he was coming up empty on the snack front, I crossed my ankles and waited for him to admit defeat. He finally turned toward me and shrugged.

"You guys need to stop living on bar food," I said with a grin. "So have you found out anything more about what Donny's been getting into with the vampires?"

He opened the fridge and withdrew two drinks—a beer for himself and a ginger ale for me. "I poked around some, but no one's talking much. The biggest thing is that they have a new HQ they're operating out of. Haven't found out where yet. Somewhere north, I gather. You watch yourself if you plan to take them on."

"Of course. I always do. Why do you look so worried?"

"In the time they've started operating in the Fringe, I've been able to learn very little. Makes me twitchy."

The lines around Rebus's eyes and mouth deepened. His discomfort with the vampire situation was more than paternal protectiveness.

He leaned against the stove and popped off the cap of his beer. "One thing I can tell you. Hit them during the day. Almost as weak as humans. Whatever you do, don't try to fight them at night."

"Okay, I won't. I'll be fine." I clapped him on the back and gathered him into a bear hug around his middle like I used to as a kid, a big, goofy grin plastered across my face. Anything to ease his mind.

"Ah! Let go before you break my ribs!" He laughed, and I released him. "I hate not knowing about things." He sighed, but the hint of a wistful smile slowly bloomed. "I know less than I need to about this situation. Whatever they're doing, I can tell you they've got outside financing. Also, Donny's in it to the teeth."

The icy bubbles of my soda soothed my throat as I gulped down a swallow. "I knew he had to have a backer. I think he may be the key to the missing-fey problem."

When he met my statement with a questioning gaze, I explained about my fruitless Caribbean adventure and the missing Dawn fey. "The thing is, he really has no reason to stir up trouble in the Dreaming. I need to figure out who this backer is."

I hesitated before continuing because I knew my next question might hit a stone wall. "From what Dúl told me, the Summer Queen seems to think her sister might be behind this. Can you tell me about the Winter Court in case I run into Nemesis's people? I wasn't kidding when I said those Dawn guys put me through it."

Rebus's face went hard, and he returned to his workspace without answering. He fit a black gear against a larger bronze one, and within moments, both glowed purple. His gaze remained fixed on the work.

"Reeb, I know you don't like to talk about your time there—"

A blazing glare flashed and silenced me but only for a second. I really didn't want to fight any more fullbloods without as much info as I could get.

"Look, I just need to know what I might be facing. Big Daddy Shadow doesn't seem to think it's her, anyway, but just in case..."

Rebus picked up a tiny screwdriver and positioned the loupe back over his eye. "If he thinks she wouldn't betray him, he's an idiot. You can't put anything past Nemesis." With a sigh, he rubbed a hand over his cheeks and chin. "She's as ruthless as it gets. In human terms, pure sociopath. When I was a kid and my talents manifested, she decided she wanted me as her weapons master. My family felt I was too young. We tried to run, hide me in another court."

"But I've never met... Oh. I'm so sorry. Let's drop it—"

He continued as if I hadn't said anything. "Only those things she needs or wants interest her. I don't see her working with vamps. They're beneath her. The Winter Queen isn't exactly humble."

As I had done since childhood, I pulled out a chair and spun it around to sit backwards on it. I picked up a small Maglite and shone it on his hands to give Reebus some extra light. "Well if not her, who else would gain anything by ramping up the fights among the siblings?"

"Pfft. You kidding? They have so many enemies in the Dreaming, kiddo. I'll do what I can to help, but you'd better hope it's not Nemesis. Think of it like this—if the Summer Queen is an arrow, the Shadow King is a poisoned dart, and the Dawn King is a loaded gun, then the Winter Queen is a nuclear bomb."

"So...you're saying I should hope I never get an invitation to high tea? Good to know."

After spending the rest of the day with my family,

I changed into stealth gear at dusk and headed toward the pier. The vampires operated out of abandoned shipping containers that sat half on land, half supported by pylons and extended over the Hudson. Across a dead-end street from the makeshift building, a burned-out warehouse provided a point of surveillance, clocking the traffic in and out of the main lab.

A few blocks away, I shifted into a mangy Rottweiler, a little foam in the corners of my mouth for good measure. My paws padded along the cracked asphalt, past the two lookouts at the corners of the burnout.

Vampire drug dealers tended to dress in order to fit in wherever they were. Hiding in plain sight. In urban areas, they wore baggy jeans hanging off their asses and oversized hoodies, but on college campuses, they looked like stereotypical frat boys. Their business took them to clubs as often as high-school hallways. These guards resembled Goth kids in tight, black gear, silver chains, and piercings.

Although they generally appeared to be humans of every color, shape, and size, their eyes identified them as vampires to those who knew what to look for—pronounced veins at the temples, blood red rims around the eyelids, and completely black pupils. They had no irises and wore dark shades all the time.

While Donny and his crew knew about my shapeshifting, I had never squared off against the vampires directly. I hoped this would work in my favor and that they wouldn't expect a shifter.

After I rounded the corner of the warehouse, past

the sentry who leaned against the building smoking a blunt, I lifted a back leg and peed against the wall before trotting toward the rear of the headquarters.

When I was sure no one had paid me any mind, I slipped into a threshold beneath a fire escape. The corroded metal ladder would unquestionably make a lot of noise, but I needed to get up on that roof. I shifted to my petite form.

In my hiding spot, I withdrew a pistol from a holster at my thigh and loaded it with a black rod. With a twist of a bolt in the middle of the rod, three barbs popped out of it—a small grappling hook. The street was deserted, so I stepped out and shot upward.

The hook landed on the edge of the roof, passed the stability test of several hard yanks and tugs, and a moment later, reeled me up. Halfway.

Snag. Shit. I mentally kicked myself for grabbing the wrong gear, namely the pistol I was supposed to have given to Rebus after the last time it malfunctioned. While the situation with Paris had distracted me when I was packing up at home, this was my own fault.

I'd have to climb the last fifty feet. *Great.*

A bottle broke some distance behind me and shattered the quiet of the night. From the front side of the building, voices reached me.

Please don't come and check.

I pulled myself up, hand over hand, toes whispering against the brick wall as they helped me balance and propel skyward.

Footsteps. The lookouts were moving around the right side of the building.

Only a few more yards to go.

The conversation was clear now. They discussed college basketball.

With one last, great heave, I pulled myself up and over the edge and flattened down against the bricks. They paused at the corner of the building.

Don't look up.

They circled the perimeter. I remained frozen until I heard them reach their original posts again. Silently, I padded across the roof, dropped down below the edge, and pulled my surveillance equipment from my pack. I hoped I hadn't been so careless with the rest of my tools.

While I had always preferred to muck up the vampires' operations from a far distance, I was prepared now to get in a little closer. They were particularly nasty after dark. No one came to this area, hence the somewhat lax security. Even the police had been paid off to stay away.

The wind whipped across the rooftop, cutting through my thermal-lined fleece. A nauseating, licorice odor with hints of copper permeated the air. Pulling a black balaclava over my nose minimized both problems.

Dúl had loaned me a pair of spectacles with short binocular lenses. After fitting them to my face, I kneeled and scoped out the area again, just to make sure there hadn't been any security upgrades like I'd seen at Donny's place.

No one on the warehouse roof. No cameras. Good to go.

Next, I pulled out a six-inch bar and pressed a tiny, metal button toward the bottom. From the top, two smaller branches popped out to form a Y. A band hooked along the side of the handle came off in order to be reattached to the top.

Once the slingshot was ready, I pulled a disc the size of a bottle cap from my pocket. The corresponding wireless earbud was already tucked in place.

I shot the disc across the street. It magnetically stuck to the side of the rusty container. Still engrossed in their conversation, the sentries didn't seem to notice the muffled plink it made against the metal. Now, everything said inside and in the surrounding area would filter directly to my ear.

It was quiet for the time being, so I huddled down and waited.

The good part of this particular stakeout was that the weather was tolerable. The bad side was that the non-activity gave me too much time to think about topics better left alone. For example, where had Paris been since he hadn't been home for a couple of days?

Was he still with the two vampire females I had heard in the background when we argued? If he was, I knew it wasn't about sex or cheating. It was all about the high. He traded his blood for drugs.

During one of his stints in rehab, he explained to

me that the vampires didn't require blood to sustain them so much as they did misery, hopelessness, and despair. Blood drinking was for a thrill, not about survival, as the legends would have us believe. Hell, they weren't even undead, although Paris never defined exactly what they *were*.

All I knew for sure was that ever since they started building their business in the Fringe, a deeper and deeper chasm had opened between Paris and me. I had hated them for making it so easy for him to abandon me.

These days, it was harder and harder to find the heady rush of feelings I had for him at the beginning. It was harder to make excuses for him or place the blame for his actions on anyone else. For a moment, I could even envision a life without him. I couldn't deny the glimmer of relief that sparked at the thought.

An odd, quick thumping sounded in my ear, thankfully bringing me out of my head. I stretched and began to position myself to peek over the side of the roof. As I moved, the microphone picked up voices, sentences broken due to their distance. The first voice was as familiar as my own, and not a surprise at all.

"... move up, kid... be good for you... new opportunities... just the beginning."

Donny. Which one of his goons was getting a promotion? The voices were closer.

Within perfectly clear range.

"Yeah, thanks. Sorry about that last situation—"

I almost threw up in my mouth.

My breath came out in little gasps. This couldn't be real. I had to pull myself together, gather information. That's why I was here. Everything else—every betraying, worst-nightmare, painful thing else—had to wait.

"You don't even worry about that. Thanks to you, our clients snagged themselves some fullbloods. And you're going to help them get as many more as they need to perfect their product. Then, we all get paid like kings." Donny laughed, snorting like the pig he is.

"They're keeping the fey here? How'd they manage to hold them?"

"Nah, kid. Not here. Those dumbass fullbloods will never find their people. They ain't even in the country. Cooling their heels across the border, from what I hear."

Canada? They had probably snagged Morgan before she even *left* the Shadow Court.

Donny continued. "But it ain't our problem where they end up. We just get the vamps through the portal and let them worry about the rest."

I wriggled onto my knees and peeked down. I had to see, to make sure my ears weren't deceiving me.

They weren't.

Donny's arm was slung around Paris's shoulder like they were the best friends in the world. Meanwhile, *my* entire universe was collapsing in on itself.

The squeal of metallic friction assaulted every nerve in my body as the warehouse door opened. Donny waved to the lookouts and then ushered Paris inside.

"The big guy left a little extra incentive for you. Come on, this way."

I had to compose myself.

It might have been easiest for me to turn into a vulture or some other large, winged creature to escape, but that would draw attention. Plus, I hated being up in the air without some kind of support—like a rope.

I rappelled down the back of the building, hands shaking with fury. *Should go in there and wrap this rope around both their necks.* I had to stop a couple of times, hugging the rope between my thighs and feet because my grip kept slipping. *Gotta get away from this.*

Too frazzled to shift, I stole through the darkness until I reached home. My body was vibrating, and it was hard to concentrate on anything, but I managed one task. I called Dúl. After a brief conversation with him, I changed into jeans, a hoodie, and a heavier fleece jacket then waited for a car to pick me up.

Those sons of bitches. The phrase, *how could he*, looped through my mind, but I kept insisting I *knew* how Paris could turn on me. He was a junkie. He'd turn on his own mother. But Donny? He was just a lowlife scumbag who brought nothing but ruin to the Fringe. Our world would be better off without him, and I couldn't wait to get my hands on him.

Chapter 10

By the time I reached the RavCorp offices, I had calmed enough to push Paris and Donny to a side compartment of my mind. Dúl met me by the elevator bank. He only hesitated for the briefest moment, and then his eyes flicked to my neck. His expression never changed, and it was only then that I remembered I had stayed in a male form since my stakeout.

He brought me to the same office I'd been in after my embarrassing defeat by the Dawn fey. His hair had that bed-messy look, which made perfect sense at 3 AM. A pair of faded jeans hugged his rear assets, and a cozy-looking cable knit sweater made me want to crawl into it, to absorb all that warmth and comfort.

As angry as I was with Paris, right now I couldn't cope with being attracted to someone else. I clamped down all my inappropriate thoughts and delivered my report.

"So, like I said on the phone, my hunch was right. It's the vampire nation. They're holding fullbloods in Canada. I can get Rebus on it and—"

"No need. Sit. Drink? Looks like you could use one."

I shook my head and lowered myself to one corner of the couch.

"After your call, I took the liberty of putting one of my best people on the trail. You forget that you have all of RavCorp's resources at your disposal. Were you able to learn how they've been getting into the Dreaming?"

My gut twisted. Donny I could gladly throw under the bus with no hesitation, but it was harder with Paris, even after what I'd learned. "Uh...yeah. Donny is the mastermind there. I heard him praising...one of his guys for helping the vampires get the fey." I watched my hands while I picked at my nails.

If Dúl found my tone subdued or my behavior odd, he didn't mention it after his long pause. He sat next to me and gently took my hands in his, linking us together, stroking the backs of my knuckles in soothing circles. Paris would have never while I was in this body.

"I see." Dúl said. "Well, we can deal with this Donny and whoever else is involved later. For now, I have a team in mind—"

"Whoa. Who said anything about a team? I specifically said, 'no team,' remember? Research is one thing." I withdrew my hands from his and shot to my feet. "I'm going in alone."

Dúl's eyes flashed as his brows drew down and together into a V. A muscle in his jaw twitched. His posture straightened, suggesting he wasn't used to having his orders challenged. "Right. Because that worked out so well for you the last time." He rose slowly.

Low blow. "I told you from the beginning, I work alone."

"And when dealing with petty changeling gangs and humans, I didn't dispute your choice. But you have to recognize that there are forces out there stronger than you. Sometimes, you're going to need help." Any hint of the former sensual or soothing timbre in his voice was gone, replaced with the bark of a commander.

I bristled and fumed, not liking the feeling of being smaller than him. So, I grew a few inches and rounded on him. "I'm aware of that. But I can't worry about anyone else's fuck-ups. Waiting for backup that never shows up or worse. And—" I pointed toward his chest. "I won't be responsible for anyone else getting hurt following my orders."

Thinking better of my overly aggressive posture, I paced the room.

Dúl watched me for a few moments, sat back down, and then relaxed into the cushions. This some-how agitated me more. But I also flopped back onto the sofa.

Silence stretched between us for long seconds as he observed me.

Eventually, he narrowed his eyes. "Are you even listening to yourself? What sense does that make? You've been rescuing kids for over a year. You take complete responsibility for them, but you don't want to tell trained professionals what to do?"

"That's different!"

The jerk responded by arching an eyebrow.

"Those kids are scared and just grateful for the promise of help, and they're right with me at all times. They just have to keep their heads down and let me work." I hooked my fingers into air quotations. "'Trained professionals,' as you call them, wouldn't be with me, and all kinds of things can go wrong, including that they might just decide to not follow instructions. I don't want that on my head."

"I see. And they call *me* a control freak."

I glared.

"You mean to tell me that in all the time Rebus was training you, the two of you never did jobs as a team?" The low pitch of his voice rankled me. I recognized the tone as one a parent might use with an unruly toddler.

My jaw ached from clenching it so hard. I squeezed the words out through gritted teeth. "'Course we did. I was a kid when he started training me. But *I* followed directions."

"Hmm..." He studied me in a way that made me feel naked. Vulnerable.

Under different circumstances, his intense gaze might have made my insides all fluttery. Now, I leaned forward with my elbows on my knees and stared at the floor. I ran my hand over the top of my head. Focusing on the sensation of my palm against my scalp.

"So what did you do that got Rebus hurt?"

My head snapped up to scowl at him, mouth open

but nothing coming out. Fingers curled into fists of righteous anger but directed at whom? I closed my mouth, relaxed my hands, and stared. Whether he knew something for sure, or if he was just playing a hunch, Dúl shouldn't have gone there. Was the paycheck worth having to deal with such a ruthless prick?

"What are you, the Shadow Court's resident shrink? It was Nat, not Rebus if you have to know. Her cover was blown, and I rushed in to help her not knowing she intended to be discovered as a distraction. Big fight. She ended up partially blind in one eye." I skewered him with my gaze, imagining hot pokers whacking him in the head. He didn't flinch. Of course not. Bottom line: *he* was paying *me*. "You want me to take a team, fine. You're the boss. You win."

He had the decency to bow his head. "It's not a contest, Umbra." There was a tenor of sadness in the way he used my birth name. "I apologize—is it all right to use that name while you're in this expression of yourself. Is it all right to use it at all?"

That was a shocker. I understood why he was asking, but the thing about my given name was that it was the only piece I had of my origins. I couldn't give it up completely. "I'd prefer you don't use it around anyone else, but you can call me that. I don't mind."

"I appreciate you trusting me with that. My point is that some situations are just too big for one individual to manage alone. And since this situation involves the Dawn Court, Orion is demanding that his people be involved too."

"Are you fucking kidding me? Please don't tell me—" I hugged my skull. This night just kept getting worse.

With a sigh, he said, "Two of the guards who captured you, and our best tech whiz. Merc, your safety—"

"Whatever. Let's just get this over with. Call me when they're here. I need some air. And to change."

Not in the mood to deal with people, I took the elevator straight to the garage and walked out of the building. My heart pounded like a war drum. Maybe I was trying to goad fate into sending me a fight, but I shifted to my female form and dared anyone to test me.

The Manhattan streets thrummed with their cabs, buses, and sirens. As I stomped along the sidewalk, a young couple approached, huddled together against the chill and chuckling in that just-got-laid way. I wanted to trip one of them. Then I scolded myself. They had done nothing but released a little more pleasure into the world. Someone should pat them on the back, but it wouldn't be me. Not tonight.

In a park overlooking the river, I found a quiet spot with a metal bench. My butt froze when I sat and drew my knees to my chin. It was just what I needed to cool my rage.

A few lights winked at me from New Jersey across the river. The air was crisp and cleared my head. The tang of the Hudson and the chop of the water soothed me. It was that time of morning, just before the sun woke, when the temperature plunged. A shiver contracted my entire body. What had happened in that room?

Dúl and I had been getting along fine. He seemed to sense that I was off balance but gave me space to deal with it while supplying a comforting presence at the same time. Then, as if a switch had been toggled, we were at each other's throats.

Why would he go out of his way to rehash my pain? He couldn't have known any details—no one did because my parents and I *never* spoke about that job. If he'd been playing a hunch, it had been a dangerous one. The last thing I needed on my mind before a mission was a past mistake that had devastating consequences. And for what? To rattle me enough to give in to his demands?

He could have just ordered me to take the team, pulled rank. Or he could have blamed it on Orion. But no, he wanted me to give in, to accept his terms without force. To submit of my own free will. What was I supposed to make of these manipulation tactics? They weren't any better than Paris's bullying or guilt-tripping.

And I had no business comparing Dúl to Paris.

The worst part was that his tactic had worked. *I* let that happen. Maybe what I had seen at the vamp lab had affected me more than I wanted to admit. Before I could delve too deeply into that thought-quicksand, my cell phone vibrated. I had been gone just over an hour.

If I knew nothing else about my team at this point, I knew they moved fast.

I approached the office on silent feet. The door was open, yet it sounded like the room was empty except for a muted clacking from inside. Before anyone could spot me, I needed to decide how to play this.

The Dawn Guards—the ones who had defeated me—would be in there. To avoid appearing weak, I stood taller and forced a neutral expression onto my face. I also added a little extra height and a touch more lean muscle to my "everyday" female frame. It couldn't hurt.

Steadying my breath, I took the last few steps and turned into the doorway.

Behind the desk, a woman who appeared to be in her mid-thirties, tapped away at a laptop keyboard. My mouth wanted to curve down into a scowl at what felt like an intrusion.

To my right, the gorgeous, dredlocked fey—machete man—and the cornrowed chick lounged on the couch.

My couch. As quickly as the words formed in my mind, I squashed them. Nothing and no one in this place belonged to me. Still, those soldiers seemed a little too comfortable.

"Where's—"

"Called away on urgent business. I am Najat of the Shadow Court. The two over there are Anton and

Betania of the Dawn Court." Lush, dark hair cascaded over Najat's shoulders, and from her profile, I could see that her nose hooked downward, beaklike. When she glanced at me over the top of wire-rimmed glasses, I realized I was staring.

My team. What was I supposed to say to them, "welcome aboard" or something equally corny? I stepped inside and linked my hands together in front of me. They were suddenly moist. That never happened.

Najat's voice had me stumped—something about the way she gently rolled her Rs and pronounced her Ls.

"Can I ask where you're from? I can't place the accent."

"The part of the Dreaming near Istanbul." As she spoke, her fingers never broke their rhythm.

Betania grinned. "You the little ninja gal knocked Anton on 'is ass wit one arm paralyzed?" Her accent reminded me of the clerk from the motel, yet she was much less irritating. Especially since she wasn't trying to grope me. Or to kill me anymore.

Now that I could see her better, I realized she appeared bi-racial with tiny curls escaping the braids at her hairline. Freckles dotted her cheeks. It was hard to remember her as a fierce fighter.

"I would be that person, yes. And sorry about that, Anton. Nothing personal."

At the opposite side of the couch, Anton studied me from head to toe with a frown but said nothing.

Betania's head rocked back as she laughed. "No

apologies. Some men like a woman can take 'em down. Me twin just got no sense of humor." *Humor* came out as *hyou-mah.*

"That scourge of yours was pretty nasty, Betania. Glad we're on the same side this time around."

"Pfft. For now." Anton's accent matched Betania's.

At least I knew he was capable of speech.

"Pay 'im no mind. He's always ill-tempered. And call me Tania."

She was definitely someone I could work with. I turned back to the last member of this crew, still entranced by her screen and keys.

"Um...Najat? Have you found any trace of them yet?"

"Hello, yes. There's been lots of activity between Poughkeepsie and Buffalo in the past few weeks—convoys and large shipments. Our target is perhaps in the Niagara Falls area. Also, there have been several disappearances... I'll need a little more time. Give me ten minutes."

I felt like I should say more, get to know these people instead of sitting in uncomfortable silence listening to Najat's keyboard. A ring and buzz sounded from the desk and made me jump. Najat tapped the phone's screen.

"Sir?"

"Merc, give Najat a list of whatever you might need and send your team with her down to the sub-level to collect the gear. Then please meet me in the aviary room. Najat can point the way."

"Sure."

When the call was disconnected, I paced the room, rattling off every item I could think of—binoculars, mics and earbuds, flash bombs, smoke bombs, pistols, daggers, picks... the list went on. It was probably over-kill, but I had no experience running a mission of this scale and would rather be over-prepared than lacking. Every now and then, Tania would "ooh" or squeal about a weapon or gadget I mentioned. Was I asking for too much? Overstepping? "Will you be able to get all that?"

"Of course." Quick as a flash, Najat's equipment was packed up, and she was out the door. The others followed her.

When I entered Dúl's larger office, the room was dim as it had been during my first visit. He stood with his back facing me, broad shoulders bunched with palpable tension beneath his sweater. One leg was bent, and he gripped the edge of the desk. Had there been a problem? An overwhelming urge seized me, and I envisioned wrapping my arms around his waist, comforting him.

Then I remembered I was still pissed off at him.

He turned and paused, like I had startled him. "You changed."

Not what I expected to hear. "Does it matter? If they can't follow me as a woman then maybe—"

He walked past me and shut the door, like I hadn't been speaking. His finger tapped the knob, as if he were deep in thought. Standing in the middle of the room, I was unsure what was happening.

"I don't normally find myself at a loss for words." He returned to his desk and leaned back against it, his arms and ankles crossed, seeming no more at ease than he had been when I arrived.

"Is something wrong?"

He gestured for me to sit next to him. I complied.

"I was unhappy with the way our last conversation ended, and I'm... disturbed about sending you off with those two. The big one in particular, I don't trust. I know you'd rather work alone, but please believe that this was necessary."

"Okay. I believe you. Earlier, why didn't you just pull rank instead of bringing up that stuff with my family? If that was some pre-mission pep talk, it was pretty fucked up. How did you even know about that?"

"I didn't. Just playing a hunch. I apologize if that hurt you. I thought facing it would give whatever happened less power over you. You're perfectly capable of functioning with and leading a team. You didn't seem aware of that."

"I guess we'll see."

"And... can you forgive me?"

My insides rippled. He shouldn't care if I forgave him or not. This was just a job, and I was still in a relationship. Yet, I suddenly didn't want to walk out of this building with bad feelings between us.

His eyes bored into mine, and a sense of urgency

infused his expression. There was a rawness, a vulnerability calling out to me. "Why?"

He stood and moved in front of me, inches separating us. "I'd rather we were on good terms before you walk into a situation where..."

Fingering a tendril of my hair, he leaned in. As if I had been magnetized, I instantly felt the need to touch him. My fingers brushed his chest.

And then his hands were at the nape of my neck and plunging into my hair. One thigh separated my knees, and he nestled between my legs.

Yes. Closer.

"Do you? Forgive me?" One thumb, tender and tentative, caressed my cheek. His fingers thrummed with warmth and longing as the other thumb lightly traced my mouth.

"Uh huh...of course." I knew where this was going and that I should stop it. But in the moment, all I wanted was to melt into that strong embrace, to forget about jobs and courts and vampires.

He closed the gap between us, and his lips glided over mine. Soft and warm, they captured my bottom lip and suckled. Dúl moaned, or maybe it was me. Warmth radiated from my belly, heating me from my core through my entire body. Time slowed, as if we had somehow slipped into the Dreaming.

My fingers played at the hem of his sweater and then underneath it, exploring the ripples of his abs. Of their own will, my legs wrapped around his, overcome with wanting to have him nearer still. He pressed in with more force, the tip of his tongue tasting and dancing with mine. Strong fingers caressed and stroked along my spine as he clutched me to him.

Lips traveling along my jawline, he kissed a path down to my neck, near my birthmark. My weak spot. I leaned back, every cell screaming for him to continue, lower.

Then the warmth of his mouth was gone, and he stopped. Breathing hard, he rested his forehead against my collarbone. His fingers gripped my waist. Desperately.

As if he thought he would never see me again.

I held him tighter, planted a kiss at his temple, stroked the pointed tip of one ear. Paris's stockier frame had always seemed like it could slip out of my grasp so easily. By contrast, Dúl's build was just as muscled but leaner, as if I could wrap my arms around him and hold on as long as I wanted. He wasn't pulling away.

Dúl groaned. "I wish I could be there with you. Ensure your safety myself. I know I have no rights ... I'm going to be in such trouble for this... and your boyfriend... Still, I needed to—"

"Shh... I could have said no. If there's a problem, it's mine to handle. Everything will be fine. I promise, and then...." I couldn't finish my sentence because I had no idea what came next. Right now, any thoughts of the future were too complicated to work through. I could only allow myself to envision as far as finding and rescuing Morgan.

As much as it pained me, I breathed in Dúl's spicy aroma once more, released him, and stood up.

"I need to get this done. We'll figure out the rest when I get back."

Interlude:
Shadow and Ice

The king's breath fogged white. New snowflakes dusted his boots.

Where was Nemesis?

Normally, she knew of any uninvited presence—sibling or not—in the Winter Court. She typically intercepted him before he could get three steps into her lands at the aspen pine that leaned slightly to the left. This showed her affection for him, and they would walk the woodland paths as they conversed.

Non-blood-relations would be slain on sight by a cadre of ghostly specters that made up the court's guard. Special treatment was reserved for the Summer Queen.

Athena would have been apprehended and imprisoned in the highest tower of the castle—windows open so the frosty winds could whip through unobstructed.

Nemesis had calmly crooned her plan for their sister. "Obviously, I can't kill her. That would be illegal. However, if she happened to fall or jump to her death because the cold was too much for her delicate constitution..."

She must know he was here. Did she expect him to trudge through the woods with spider-like branches of barren foliage snatching at his head with each step? What could the Winter Queen be angry about this time? Not that it took much to incur her wrath.

The king stepped onto the path, soggy pine needles mushy under his feet. The temptation was strong to abandon this fool's quest. Even if Nemesis would commit treason against the realm, which he didn't doubt, she'd slit her wrists before allying with "lesser beings."

Still, the king marched on.

His elder sister and eight white-clad soldiers met him at the castle's crystalline gate. Eight spears of ice pointed at his heart.

"Why have you come here?" Her voice rang out, deep and clear, into the frigid air.

Odd.

In addition to the loud volume, he had never known her to do or say anything before so many witnesses. Perhaps the cold had finally frozen her reason.

It had taken her humor ages ago when Athena's whining combined with bad luck to give Nemesis rule over the coldest parts of the Dreaming. Having the largest geographic area did nothing to appease her.

"My sister. There is a private matter we need to discuss. Might we walk as we speak?"

Azure eyes bored into him. Nemesis's pure white hair flowed over shoulders that drew back, prouder than any soldier's. A labyrinthine mask of wrinkles obscured any definition in her facial features.

When she replied, her voice, which had never been warm but also never held any particular malice toward him, came out in a low snarl. "No."

Stunned, the king blinked. What was happening here? "Nemesis, this is an urgent family matter, and—"

"Leave my lands before I order my guards to run you through. And never step foot here, uninvited, again... Brother." Her sentence ended on her usual purr, but there it was again—the slight bite of her words twisted with a touch of threat.

He was unafraid, certainly not of her warriors. He knew as well as she did that he could teleport them to a Shadow realm where they'd all go mad until death claimed them.

What alarmed the Shadow King was the sudden change in his sister. That puzzle would be best solved another time. With a nod, he stepped backward, pulling the shadows to him from the surrounding tree line. Before the darkness cocooned him, he noticed a subtle, nearly imperceptible curve at the corners of his sister's mouth. If he hadn't noticed anything amiss, this solidified his apprehension.

Nemesis never smiled.

Chapter 11

Dúl wasn't fooling around when he said we'd have everything we needed. I didn't ask how a surveillance/security company had a virtual arsenal of automatic weapons and military-grade armor, in addition to the most wonderful array of stealth and spying gear I'd ever seen. I had a few Rebus-made toys that might come in handy too.

I didn't want any guns, but he insisted I wear Kevlar beneath daytime camos. "The Shadow King would be furious if anything happened to you."

No argument from me on that point.

There were also throwing daggers, throwing stars, grenades...it was like stepping into a video game. One that I might not come out of in one piece.

Once we were all decked out in combat gear—even Najat—a car transported us to Westchester Airport where we boarded the RavCorp jet. And to think, not long ago I had gotten to my last job by entering a strip club, starting a fight with one of Donny's thugs, and being slung over the brute's shoulder before he tossed me into a cell.

How could I go back to my former life when this was all done?

Once on the plane, Najat projected images of our destination onto a pull-down screen. A biotech facility had been completed about six months ago at the outskirts of a city called St. Kat's in Ontario. Some digging revealed that the company was bogus and traced back to an intricate web of fake corporations. One name came up in a cross-reference search: Genesin Fantine, who also appeared on Homeland Security watch lists and had a loose connection to Donny.

Najat had thermal images and schematics that blew my mind. "How'd you get those?" I asked, stunned.

"The ravens can get in quite close."

We landed at Niagara Airport, about fifteen minutes away from Fantine, International. No limo waited this time. Instead, a battered white van sat behind the end of the tarmac, near the hangar. Although the outside of the vehicle looked a mess, the inside had screens, speakers, computers, a mini refrigerator, and even a coffee maker.

I drove as Najat navigated me toward a wooded area bordering a golf course. That was about the only civilized area nearby, aside from a couple of farms spread far apart.

We pulled in, hid the van as best as we could, and listened to Najat's explanation.

"The compound is on the other side of these woods, but we won't be able to get any closer in the van without raising suspicion. You'll have to approach on foot."

"Tania and I will scout ahead, get a feel for this place. Anton, keep an eye on the trees. We don't want to find out they do patrols or something."

Our fitted, thermal fatigues were warm enough to withstand the frigid, early-morning wind as we snuck through the forest. A ten-foot fence with barbed wire at the top circled the perimeter. Was that to keep intruders out or someone else—like the missing fey—in?

The blueprints had marked several offices and two observation rooms on the main level that looked down into two large procedure rooms. The first below-ground level held the labs. Najat pulled up digital images of twenty heat signatures inside—fifteen vampires and five humans—and a large area in the sub-basement giving off some serious magical energy.

Keeping low and moving silently, Tania and I crept around to the gate, the only way into or out of the enclosure. We lay in the brush, frost crunching beneath us, and watched through binoculars.

A small guard shack was just outside the gate. No one had surfaced yet. Vampires can move around during the day if they cover up, but even then, they stay out of direct light as much as possible.

"What ya make of dem pictures, especially the big one underground?" Tania swept her gaze up toward the roof of the building. "All clear up there."

"I don't know, but my guess would be that's where

they're keeping the fey, under some kind of magic sup-pression. I'd love to get eyes inside. Weird how quiet this place is since we know there are bodies moving around in there. Seems they're pretty confident. Not expecting us. That helps."

"Why not just turn into a fly or somet'ing? You're the shifter, yeah?"

I couldn't help but smile at her. "I can't turn into anything so small anymore. Not since I was a kid. You don't do much surveillance, do you?"

"Nah. King calls, I fight. Lord Orion isn't one for sneakin' around. He leaves that to your Shadow Lord."

"Not my anything lord. This is only a one-time job."

When she opened her mouth to say more, I held one finger to my lips. She placed her thumb and fore-finger together at one corner of her mouth and drew them across the seam before quieting down and re-focusing her attention on our target.

Two hours later, I almost wished she hadn't. Noth-ing was going on in there, which worried me, but at the same time, I gave up hope that we'd get any more information than we already had. Just as I was about to signal to Tania that it was time to return to the others, a large object thudded against my shoulder. Talons gripped me.

"What the—"

A raven. The bird opened its beak and spit out two pea-sized objects. It then pecked toward my ear. *Ugh.* I wiped the little sphere off on my jacket, put it in my ear, and gave the other to Tania.

Najat's voice piped into my head. "Best not to use these too much. I don't think we're being monitored, but you never know. There's a truck approaching from the west, heading for the gate."

"Okay." I made eye contact with Tania and saw that she understood. Then bringing two pairs of binoculars to our eyes, we waited some more.

Finally, our patience paid off. A white box truck rolled up to the gate, and two vampires emerged from the shack in military-style black uniforms. Both had semiautomatic pistols strapped to their hips.

The truck's driver—another vampire dressed in khaki coveralls—spoke to the others for a moment. They all went to the back, and the driver lifted the door. Over a dozen people, bound with plastic zip ties and linked together like chattel, lined the sides of the truck while some slumped in the center of the truck's bed.

"Mighty Orion," Tania whispered. "Dey can't be all fey."

"Nope. I count three changelings. The rest are humans. Probably blood patrons—that's what they call the people they feed from." *People like Paris.* I took a deep breath to clear my head.

Her face crumpled, and she looked like she might be sick. "What kind of monsters do such a t'ing?"

Answering would just upset her more, so I observed in silence. These patrons—if that was their purpose—complicated things. They weren't my mission, but I couldn't just leave them to be convenient snack food for a bunch of drug-dealing fiends.

"We've seen enough. Let's head back." A plan took shape.

As we approached the van's hiding spot, making sounds to avoid startling Anton, his hand flew to the machete on his back, and he crouched into a defensive stance.

"It's us." I came out from behind the trees a second later, and he relaxed.

In the van, Najat was just as we'd left her.

"Thanks for the heads up about the truck. We might have missed it." I waited for Anton and Tania to join us before continuing. "Okay, there's a slight complication, but it might work in our favor." Tania and I told the others about the captives. "So, if we release them, they can distract the vamps, or at least some of them, which will make it easier for us to get to our target. Tania, you stay back with Najat—"

"No."

I turned to Anton. "Excuse me?"

"Those people are not our mission. Three of us should go in, free the fey, get out." His scowl told me he was about to dig in. "We don't deal with half breeds and human scum."

Tania rolled her eyes at him.

"Maybe you'd have an easier time following my orders if I looked different?" I shifted, shrinking my hair to a buzzed length on my head flattening my chest more, stretching and molding my features until I was in a form somewhere between my male and female bodies. "Is this better?" This was new for me, and it felt comfortable.

"I don't care what you look like—you're not qualified to give anyone orders."

"Look, who's going to cover Najat? We can't leave her out here on her own. If one of them comes through here—"

"No one's patrolled since we've been here."

"And second, using the others as a distraction—people who will fight their captors—will give us less vampires to deal with."

"Fighting the enemy is not a problem for a Dawn Soldier. Sneaking, hiding behind others—that is the Shadow way. I don't expect someone like you to understand honorable tactics."

Tania covered her face and groaned.

Before I could respond, Najat did. "Merc was put in charge for a reason. Your king ordered you to do as she says—I heard him. Wait, do I still call you 'she?' I've never met a shifter."

"'They,' actually. Thanks for asking."

"Lord Orion would agree with me. *They* got captured last time."

For someone who thought himself so honorable, he sure didn't seem to have a problem striking below the proverbial belt.

The situation was spiraling out of my control. They

both had valid points. I had been put in charge, but I had also fucked up the last time I met these team members. Why would they trust me? But which one was more right? This team thing had been a bad idea from the start. Dissent, disobedience, attitude—these were the issues that had worried me to begin with.

"So, you intend to launch a three-person, frontal assault against at least twenty enemies. Am I hearing that correctly? And we should leave the last team member to fend for herself? That's your 'honorable' solution?"

"We meet our enemies face-to-face." He crossed his arms over his chest, not swayed by logic.

Maybe that's why Orion hasn't beaten his brother. If this soldier's attitude was any sign, Orion's stubbornness and self-righteousness were a major weakness.

"Fine. You want to call the shots, be my guest."

"Merc—" Najat said.

"It's fine. We'll likely get ourselves killed," I paused to glare at Anton, "but don't worry, Najat; *I* won't leave you out here totally defenseless."

Before the team had reassembled, Dúl had given me a talisman—a miniature onyx raven with runes carved across its unfurled wings. It was meant to open a portal to transport us all back to New York once we had successfully completed the mission. I handed it to Najat.

"If there's trouble, you bug out and arrange for the jet to be on standby. We'll find our way to the airport."

"You can't—" she began.

"Sure, I can, and I've had about enough arguing for one day, so just take it."

She did, and the rest of us prepared to implement Anton's foolish plan.

Or so he thought.

Before leaving the van, I bent and whispered to Najat. In response, she pointed at her laptop screen. With a nod, I patted her on the shoulder and headed out after the others.

Chapter 12

"It's not too late to switch gears."

I had double checked my daggers and tools. A niggling feeling crept down my spine. This was all wrong, but how was I supposed to make Anton comply? Even if I physically forced him somehow, he still wouldn't agree with my plan. There would be a risk of him going off on his own and ruining everything. At least this way, we were together, for all the good it would do.

"You know as well as I do that you are no leader," Anton sneered. "I can see it in your eyes. No faith in your own ability, and with good reason. Follow our lead and learn from the professionals."

"Whatever, dude. My lack of faith is in this stupid idea, not in myself. But if you insist, go on."

Anton ignored his sister as she stared at him with sadness in her eyes. I had no siblings that I knew of, but it must have been difficult to watch someone she loved vehemently sticking to a path of self-destruction. That much I could relate to.

The midday sun was high overhead as we made our way toward the gate. Another bad choice. Fortunately, the guardhouse had only one window in front with the blinds drawn and a door on the left side nearest the gate. A camera on the roof most likely sent video directly to the vampires inside the shed.

I gestured to the raven perched on a branch overhead as I popped a stick of Rebus's gum in my mouth. The scavenger landed on my wrist, claws scraping into my skin. When the piece was a nice-sized wad, I pointed to the camera, whispered my instructions to the bird, and held the sticky ball in my opposite palm.

The raven took it and flew over the guardhouse. It swooped, almost touching the roof, and stuck the gum on top of the camera. The substance seeped down over the lens.

"Clear!" I crouched and prepared to charge.

Anton rushed the shack from the left. As I ran forward, I pulled a dagger from my belt. When the first vampire stepped out, I guess to check why their video had gone dark, my dagger spiraled through the air, end over end, until it lodged in his eye socket. He cried out and dropped like a stone. A thick, inky substance oozed from his eyes and mouth. *Gross!*

All around us, the air was suddenly filled with the sound of a child's laughter. I scanned the area. There was no one else around. My skin crawled.

Tania had followed close behind me, whip glowing in her hand. The second vamp lunged from the guardhouse. She lashed at him. The tails wrapped around his throat. Using her fey strength, she tried to yank him forward, but his muscle matched hers. Instead, he gripped the whip ends and reeled *her* in.

Joyful giggling grew louder. *What the hell?* I had no idea where the sound came from or what it was. I wanted to seek out the source, but there was no time for it.

Anton came up behind Tania's vampire and bashed him with the hilt of the machete. Once the enemy was down, Anton delivered a killing stroke across the bloodsucker's throat. The body lay motionless. A second later, those red-rimmed eyes blinked, and the vamp grinned.

Without thinking, I snatched my dagger from the first vampire's corpse, now shriveling to a desiccated husk, and threw it at the second vamp. The blade again lodged in the eye, and the vamp dropped, the same substance seeping from his eyes and mouth.

My stomach churned as I watched. I noticed four white fangs next to the first vamp's head. It looked like they had been plucked neatly out of his mouth.

The childlike laughter that had filled the air faded to silence. A chill rippled through me from head to toe from the creepiness of it, but I shook it off. I filed the sound away to process later.

"Well...that happened." I smiled sarcastically at Anton. "So much for meeting the enemy head-on." I turned to Tania. "We have to take out the eyes for them to stay down. I doubt the ones inside will go down so easily, so be careful. They're stronger out of the sun."

Without pausing for a response, I hurried inside the tiny shack and pressed the gate button. When I exited, the three of us stashed the bodies back in the house.

We raced across the fifty yards between the gate and the shorter side of the L-shaped building. The driveway continued forward toward the main door at the longer side of the structure.

Standing under a deep eave, I wiped the dagger I had recovered on my pants leg. I would have been shaken if I had killed a human, a changeling, or a fey. But a vampire? A dark sense of satisfaction snaked through me like a shadow.

I moved behind my teammates. "Hold still." Now that I had seen one of the vampire guards up close, I could mimic his form. It only had to be good enough to get me through the door.

By the time I finished, Tania's jaw hung slack. "Mighty Orion! I don't think I'll ever get used to seeing you do that."

"Come on, you two. Walk with your hands behind your backs like you're being restrained."

"What is this? This wasn't part of the plan."

I had no more time for Anton's nonsense. "We're improvising. I agreed to go in through the front, not to be an idiot about it. We want to delay raising an alarm as long as we can, so just shut up and move."

Before he could argue, Tania hissed at him. "Just do it, Anton!"

With a glower, he marched forward, and she

followed. They concealed their glowing weapons be-hind their backs. I held their arms as if I had appre-hended them outside.

A pretty, red-headed receptionist with the signa-ture crimson rings around her eyes sat at a long, high desk on the other side of the doors. I waved, and she nodded. The glass barrier slid open. We approached her. At the same time, I tapped Tania on the arm, willing her to understand my signal.

The greeter opened her mouth with a smile. In an instant, Tania's hand glowed and a luminescent ball of water shot forward. Nothing happened. The recep-tionist didn't melt into a puddle. Her face just dripped water as if she had been hit with a kid's water balloon. A slow smile stretched her face.

Next, the whip lashed out and around the recep-tionist's throat. Futilely, she grabbed at the tails with one hand. The other hand lifted as if she was waving.

She *was* waving.

I turned. Over the door, a small camera watched our every move. Too late, Tania wrenched the vamp's neck, snapping it with a sharp yank of the whip. With-out missing a beat, she bashed the whip's handle into the receptionist's eyes.

"We're about to have company. Hold them here," I said in a rush.

I was already moving down the corridor when I glanced around. My team had positioned themselves back-to-back as vampires streamed out of an office. Anton had wanted a fight. Now he had one.

About halfway down the hall, I came to a steel wall and double doors. I scanned it for the lock. It appeared to be a bolt mechanism requiring a heavy-duty key. If the replacement lock pick Rebus had given me didn't work, we were all screwed.

From the front of the building, the first gunshots rang out. I heard lots of incoherent shouts and then a scream. Tania. I resisted the impulse to rush back to the fight.

I plucked the pick from my belt and crouched to jam it into the keyhole. It glowed bright purple. There was a loud crack, and the light faded. I pulled on the handle, and the doors swung open. Fifteen faces snapped toward my direction.

"I'm here to help. You can stay and be lunch, or you can fight your way out."

The prisoners didn't wait for any further explanation. They jumped to their feet. I led the way back to the entrance. My heart leapt into my throat.

Anton's sword sliced an arc around him, taking the heads of two vampires attacking from his sides. Apparently, decapitation worked on them. A third leapt onto his back. Dripping fangs tore into the side of Anton's throat, ripping a mortal gash into his neck.

Tania was pinned down behind the reception desk, a bloodied Glock in one hand. When she saw her brother, she screamed, pumping a barrage of bullets into the face of the enemy who had claimed the warrior. Anton stumbled backward. He dropped to the floor next to her. Bright blue blood, the same color that his weapon had glowed, poured from his wound.

The freed captives rushed toward the vampires. Some picked up weapons from corpses, others attacked with their hands. A few made a break for the doors, leaving the fight to the more capable ones.

Three of my daggers flew and skewered their marks. I threw myself behind the desk to join my team. My eyes connected with Tania's teary ones. I had to get her out of there or all of this would be for nothing. I reached over to the receptionist's still skeleton and ripped a strip of fabric from her red pencil skirt. After tying it around Anton's wound, I slung his opposite arm around my shoulder and practically dragged him to his feet.

The prisoners had been all but destroyed. We had to escape. Now.

"Tania, follow me!"

She helped me with him, and we made our way down the short hall to the holding room where I'd found the humans and changelings. At the back of the room was the door I knew would be there.

"This way."

"Not me," Anton wheezed. His breathing was labored. He had slumped to the floor by the double doors.

"Come on, we can deal with that wound once we get past this room. Just a little farther."

"No. You go. Finish the mission. I will stop them

from getting past this room." He held up a blue, egg-sized object.

We had to go, but I didn't want to leave him behind. I couldn't do it to Tania, whose tears mixed with his blood to soak the makeshift bandage around his neck.

"Anton—"

Tania's gaze shot toward me, her eyes blazing, stopping whatever I was going to say. She held her brother's face in both her hands, planted a hard kiss on his forehead, and said, "You honor us with your sacrifice. We will avenge you, brother."

They clasped hands in a soldier's grip one last time before he pushed her away. "Go."

She ran at me and shoved me toward the stairway leading down to the sub-levels.

Feet pounding through the first basement level, we passed two areas that resembled operating rooms. A glance up showed the observation areas on the main floor. But where was the outlet to the next level down?

We were almost at the end of the long side of the L when I heard rapid gunfire. Except it wasn't around me. It came through my earpiece.

No. No!

"Najat? Najat, can you hear me?" I couldn't care less if we were being monitored.

"Merc, yes, I'm here." In the background, I could still hear her fingers tapping on the keyboard. "I'm setting the van to self-destruct before I open the portal." She sounded just as composed as if she were telling me my tea was ready. If I made it out of here, I definitely wanted this fey as an ally.

"Get out of there, now! Just remember to have the jet on standby for us if we make it out!"

"If? What's—"

"When. I meant when. Just go!"

The shots grew louder, but then the click-clacking stopped, and the connection went silent. I hoped that meant she'd made it to safety.

Tania and I reached the end of the hall. There was another set of bolted, steel doors. She flopped to the floor next to them, panting. I paused to listen before pulling out my lockpick and shifting out of this vampire body.

The silence was unnerving, almost as if the building had been evacuated. I glanced down at Tania. Her face was tear-stained, her head banging lightly against the door.

"I-I'm so sorry about your brother."

"You should be." Her glare forced me to take a step back.

"Excuse me? It was *his* idea to fight our way in. *He* didn't want to skulk and sneak around."

"And he wasn't the leader of this mission!" She closed her eyes for a moment like she was praying for strength or meditating, and then pressed up to her feet. Her hands were balled into tight fists. "Like Najat said, you were chosen for a reason. Not me, not Najat, not Anton. You. And you let him push you into doing the wrong thing. You knew it was a bad plan, but you went with it anyway."

"What was I supposed to do? Physically force him to do what I said?" I fought not to raise my voice and give away our position, if we hadn't been discovered already.

"No. You were supposed to do what you did at the end. Ignore his bullshit and assert yourself. He was a soldier. Trained to follow a leader. And he did, once you started acting like one."

Damned if she wasn't one hundred percent right. She met my gaze, and then her face crumpled. Tension pulled her features together as if they would all implode into a black hole of self-destruction. But instead of shattering, she scrubbed her face harshly with her hands and composed herself.

"What's next?" she asked with no malice or anger, just focused determination.

"Your brother sacrificed himself so we could finish the job. That's what's next."

I popped the lock with my pick as she slapped a new clip into her gun. We stepped through the doors.

The stench was a punch to the gut. Decomposing flesh would have been appetizing compared to this odor. Tiled walls curved around two open walkways opposite each other as a river of opaque liquid flowed between them.

"Don't slip," I told Tania as I stepped onto the path that was slick with some unseen substance. A bright, green light up ahead provided enough ambient light to guide us forward. I felt a tap on my arm and stopped to turn. Tania handed me her whip, which gave off its own aura.

As I took my next step forward, a rumble ran through the tunnel followed by the ground shaking. Droplets of condensation splattered down on our heads as we hugged the wall trying not to fall into the muck.

"What was that?" Tania's voice quivered.

"Explosion? Anton's grenade? No idea. More concerned with what's up ahead and what might show up behind us."

We picked up the pace. In a minute, we reached a stone platform raised up in the middle of the tunnel. The sewage flowed underneath it. At each of the three corners of the dais facing me, clear globes the size of softballs with dark smoke swirling around inside were mounted on long staves. Within the boundary of these torch-like setups, a huge cage of green light held a solitary figure.

She had on a raggedy, gray tee and dirty sweats that were several inches too short. But Morgan's face was unmistakable.

"You? He sent *you*. Bastard." Morgan's gaze bore into me like a blast of acid, and it was clear her words were directed at me.

Chapter 13

Not exactly the welcome one would expect when rescuing an abductee. *What a bitch.* Life never failed to surprise. What had I ever done to this woman other than risk my life to free her?

Swallowing my personal opinion of my client, I focused on our task. "Morgan? What happened to the other fey? Were they kept with you?"

"Idiots thought they could fight their way to freedom." She waved her hands in a mocking gesture. "Their throats were torn out, and the vampires feasted on them." She drawled and pronounced her words in a proper, "old-money" tone, just above a bored whisper.

I wondered if I had sustained a concussion without realizing it because this was becoming surreal. "Um, okay. What do you know about these orbs? Do you know if there's a control somewhere?"

"Imbecile. They're magic inhibitors. The mist churning inside is my magic, drained from me. If you merely break them, my magic floats out of this tunnel with the rest of the piss and scum. I imagine *you* must feel right at home here."

Oh-kay. I'd dealt with snotty clients before. This one wouldn't break me. Anyone under such an enormous amount of stress would lash out. Still, she could stand to dial it down several notches.

"Keep being such a bitch, and those orbs might suddenly roll off their bases by accident. We're here to *help* you. Now what can you tell me about this cell?"

Morgan scowled at me for a long time, her nose wrinkling as if she had just noticed the stink of this place.

Tania answered. "I've seen something similar before. To...er...detain Shadow prisoners. Ours would be blue, but no Court's magic is green."

"Got it. How would someone disable yours?"

"I've no idea. Never seen it happen."

Our walkway was about two feet wide. A five-foot wide river of sewage flowed between us and the platform. Another two feet spanned between the platform's edge and the light cage.

"So, what happens if someone touches the bars?"

A mischievous grin blossomed on Tania's face. "Don't."

I actually laughed. "Great." I turned back to Morgan. "Hey, how did they get your magic out of you in the first place?"

She rolled her eyes and sat on the cell floor. "As I was restrained, they forced the spheres between my hands and did a spell. If I can make contact with the spheres, I should be able to reverse the spell. But the only way to do that would be to incinerate myself by touching the bars of light. These brutes aren't without a sadistic sense of humor."

Just then, a faint thudding sounded overhead. I couldn't hear feet or voices yet, but they had to be coming.

Now or never. I brought the toes of one foot just past the edge of the walkway and braced the other foot against the tunnel wall. Eyes locked on the nearest staff, I rocked back and forth once...twice.... And then I leapt over the sludge.

One foot landed squarely on the platform. The other slipped. I tottered, arms flailing. I reached and connected with the thin pole. My balance returned, but the globe wobbled on its base.

"Don't let it break!" Morgan was as close as she dared to the glowing barrier.

Without even realizing it, I released the pole just as the ball landed in my palm with a light smack. My hand bobbed a couple of inches from the warm sphere's unexpected weight. When it left the base, a corner of the cell disappeared.

"Here!" I tossed it to Morgan, who caught if deftly and began to speak words to reverse the spell.

Another thundering crash, this one much closer.

I tore around the edges of the platform, retrieving the spheres. Morgan had withdrawn her magic from three of them when I heard the first shout and a boom.

"Jump!"

Morgan seemed about to argue then took a running

start across the dais and flung herself across the gap. Tania caught her before she crashed into the wall. I tossed the last globe over and hurled myself behind Morgan. Then, the three of us sprinted to the end of the tunnel—the only way out.

I took the lead. Holding my breath, I hopped into the frigid sludge. It was only about waist high, but that was no comfort. Grit from the wastewater clung to my skin, and although I knew it had to be my imagination, I could swear things moved down there.

Morgan hesitated again before squeezing her eyes shut and plunging in. Tania brought up the rear.

The tunnel fed into a pitch dark pipe, forcing us to crouch, submerging ourselves until the water reached our necks. The reek was dizzying. My head pounded. We had gone a few feet into the pipe when the loud pops and twangs of ricocheting bullets spurred us on faster.

Gruff voices shouted, but they didn't seem to be following. I knew they could see us. Why weren't they pursuing?

Silently, we waded through the sewer for what seemed like an eternity until a horizontal bead of light appeared up ahead. I thought to warn the others except I couldn't force my mouth open. Swallowing literal shit had never been part of the deal.

My muscles burned and cramped from being hunched for so long. Finally, we reached the end of the pipe and could stand. Clean air diluted the stench but not by much. Daylight beckoned to us. I nearly collapsed with relief when we reached the end.

An open gully continued downhill from the mouth of the tunnel. There must be a pond or some other type of treatment facility at the bottom. But we weren't heading that way. We needed to get up onto the bank and into the woods.

Every instinct compelled me to get out of this nastiness as fast as I could.

I paused to listen. All was quiet, except for the slightest rustle of movement in the grass up and to my right.

If I were the vampires, and I knew there was only one way my prey could exit, would I bother to dirty and exhaust myself? Or would I just send someone to execute them as soon as their heads poked out?

Turning, I pulled Tania to me and moved as close as I could to Morgan. "Ambush. Can you finish reversing the spell? Quietly?" Maybe my whispers wouldn't carry outside.

She glowered but nodded. Seconds later, the black smoke seeped out of the sphere, engulfing her hands and arms, fusing into her chest and head.

"Do you have a weapon?" I mouthed.

Morgan held out her right hand. With the left, she withdrew a truly beautiful dagger, ten inches long with a gentle S curve to the blade and made of a single piece of a metal I couldn't identify. The matte black blade slid right out of her skin. Something about it sent a strange tingle through me, as if it held some kind of power.

Using hand signals, I mimed that I would go up the right bank while they scaled the left. Closing my eyes for a last, silent prayer, I held up my left hand to count down. One...two....

With a battle roar, Tania and I burst out of the pipe together and attacked the banks.

Four vamps faced me with surprised expressions. A fast assessment told me that they seemed to have abandoned the guns. Maybe they figured we were so outnumbered, they wouldn't need weapons.

It might have been a valid point.

I snagged the closest ankle and wrenched it toward me as I dug into the grass and mud, using the vampire as an anchor to pull myself up. On his way down, I smashed my fist into his face.

The childlike giggle from earlier returned, surrounding us all, faint and distant. It seemed to only show up when there were vamps around.

I reached back to my waistband for one of my daggers, ignoring the muck coating the hilt. In a swift move, I withdrew it and stabbed up into the next enemy's groin.

The phantom voice shrieked, gleeful.

Climbing higher as my enemy fell to his knees, I sliced into another's hamstring. He didn't give in so easily. He grabbed the back of my jacket, hauled me up in the air, and slammed me down. Dirt and grass filled my mouth.

Landing knocked the wind out of me. A boot smashed into my ribs. The vampire who had thrown me sent a kick into my kidney. I jabbed my blade into his calf. The already-injured vamp howled. Releasing the knife, I grabbed his boot with both hands and twisted. He toppled and slid down the incline. With a screech, Morgan appeared, leaped down, and finished him off.

A hand grabbed me by the throat and lifted me. All my brain could register were bared fangs, sharp claws digging into my scalp, and the crimson-rimmed eyes of my enemy. With a menacing grin, he drew me in, eyeing the pulsing artery in my neck. I tried to pull my knees up between us. No good. Even in the daylight, my arm strength was no match for his preternatural ability.

The psycho laughter amplified. Whatever was pro-ducing it seemed to get off on witnessing chaos.

I stopped resisting, and the spirit-giggle receded.

When the vamp and I were nose-to-nose, close enough to kiss, I reached up and plugged both my thumbs into his eyes as deep as they would go. He dropped me, but I held on, the jelly-like surface of his eyes slick over my skin.

His claws raked into my arms. He went slack as the ichor flowed from his eyes and mouth. I thrust him away from me and reached for another blade to deal with the others. With a curse, I realized my daggers were all gone.

Cold metal slapped into my palm.

The dagger that Morgan had pulled from her arm. It warmed to my touch, and a pulse of energy traveled up my arm. Even covered in crap, never had a blade felt so perfect in my hand, like an extension of me instead of a tool.

"Finish them and get me out of this hellhole." Morgan trudged away.

I destroyed the eyes of the other vampires I had disabled. The razor-sharp blade moved through skin and bone alike as if slicing water. Their bodies, along with the ones Tania had killed, all oozed and shriveled, leaving the molasses-like muck and several sets of fangs behind.

As much as I wanted to lie down in the cool mud and rest, we weren't safe yet. I had no illusions that the vampires who had chased us down to the sewer wouldn't show up to check on their buddies eventually.

I jogged past Morgan deeper into the cover of the trees. Now that I had a moment to process our location, I saw that we were in the surrounding woods about a few hundred yards from the guardhouse.

Once I determined that we were all relatively okay, I paused to catch my breath against a tall oak. "We've got a pretty long hike back to the airport. If Najat got away, she would have let them know to ready the plane."

"Hike?" Morgan sneered at me as if I was the only one here covered in shit and mud. "I don't 'hike.' Ignorant half breed."

I didn't have the energy to listen to any of her other mutterings or to fight with her, so I reverently cleaned the dagger. "Thanks for letting me borrow this." Reluctantly, I handed it back to her. "You have a better idea for getting us home, your uppitiness?"

Beside Morgan, Tania chuckled. A pang of guilt and sadness shot through me. Had I stepped up sooner, her brother might be alive. Still, I was pleased that she'd made it out with us. We could probably be friends if she could ever forgive me.

Morgan huffed. "Come closer, impudent beast. I've half a mind to leave you here, but the king would flay me if anything happened to his pet."

I moved nearer to her. "What are you—"

Before I could finish my sentence, a dark orb appeared and expanded between Morgan's hands, first the size of a golf ball, then the size of a basketball. Finally, it ballooned around the three of us, swallowing us in darkness.

We appeared in a bedroom the size of my entire apartment. A four-poster, king-sized bed seemed small in the spacious chamber filled with a chaise lounge, dressers, a huge vanity, and two other couches. In the center of the black, tiled floor, a tiger skin rug seemed to snarl.

"You will clean yourself and put on something presentable before we continue on to meet his highness." Morgan gave Tania a snarling glance. At least her meanness wasn't restricted to me. "I suppose we can't send you back to your Court in this state. I'll have someone find you suitable clothing as well."

A few minutes after she left, two Shadow fey came in and showed us to a large hall with four marble shower stalls. The water was only lukewarm. Either someone needed to teach these fullbloods about water heaters, or Morgan wanted to make sure I wouldn't be too comfortable. Whatever the reason was, I was just grateful to get clean.

As the slime and filth spiraled down the drain, it took with it all the tension and adrenaline I had been holding in since we had left New York. Pungent soap reminded me of tea tree oil and cleansed the last traces of dirt from under my nails. I remembered the feel of the Shadow dagger in my hand. I wondered if I could work out a deal with Dúl to get me another one.

Within a second, my mind leaped down the rabbit hole of Dúl-themed fantasies. I remembered the precise pressure of his fingers on my face. While I shampooed, it was his fingers massaging my scalp. The memory of his spicy scent overpowered any other aromas. How would he greet me when I returned? More importantly, how would I respond? The mission had allowed me to push aside how complicated things had gotten between us. I wouldn't be able to hide from the choice waiting for me once I got back.

When I finished showering, I found that someone had left us clothing. Tania was given loose black pants and a matching kimono-type tunic. I received similar attire—about two sizes too big for me. I could have knotted, folded, and tucked the clothing to fit this form, but screw Morgan. I had no intention of meeting royalty dressed like an orphan from a Dickens novel. Instead, I adjusted my body to fit the clothes, I took my male form—not too muscular, but taller and broader. I kept my face.

I quickly detangled my long curls with my fingers and let it hang wild, dripping water down my back.

We were led down a stone hall into another chamber where Morgan waited. She wore a black, calf-length, silk dress with dainty slippers. It clung to every curve and contour of her figure, and I had a second to regret not transforming myself into a shapely female form. If she was surprised at my appearance, she didn't show the slightest flinch.

Now that I could study her, she was what I'd call striking, but not pretty. If anything, her combination of flawless skin, huge dark eyes, full rosy lips—all those things typically would have categorized her as classically attractive. Her constant bitchiness ruined the effect.

With a wave and a word, she opened a swirling black portal and gestured Tania through it. "Najat will meet you on the other side in the Waking and arrange for your transport back to your Court."

Tania reached up and pulled me into a hug that I gladly returned.

"I'm sorry again, about—"

Her eyes were watery as she shushed me. "All in the line of duty." Sucking in a deep breath, my new friend stepped into the vortex, I had a strange feeling our paths might cross again. That would be a good thing.

Once the first portal closed, Morgan opened a second one and pointed me toward it. I stepped in. Soon after, I had to shut my eyes. The portal spun me around until I felt like I'd gone through the spin cycle of an industrial washing machine.

We stepped into Dúl's office—the cozy room I'd become so fond of. Why were we here? I patted my hair and straightened the knots and tucks of my clothes.

He stood behind the desk talking on a cell phone. When he saw us, his mouth gaped. "I'll call you back." He dropped the device to the desk before hurrying around to sweep me into an unexpected and crushing embrace. In this shape, I figured he'd pat me on the back or give me a bro-ish handshake. Yet he held me to him like he saw no difference.

Paris would have scowled and refused to touch me until I changed into someone that suited him better.

"When Najat showed up...I was about to get on a plane myself...."

"They're fine, my lord. Three of us escaped. The other Dawn soldier didn't make it. I can report to your brother if you like."

Dúl loosened his hold on me, pinched the bridge of his nose, and sighed. "Yes, Morgan. Please do. I'm relieved to have you back unharmed." If his tone were any colder, ice would have formed on her knitted eyebrows. He didn't even glance her way, keeping his eyes trained on mine. I wanted to throw myself back into his embrace, but something in Morgan's last words stopped me.

She said, "Thank you, *my lord*. I'm eager to get back to work. I'm sure there's plenty needing my attention, as I'm not required here." She turned, walked toward the door, and paused before opening it. Still facing it, she said, "And thank you, Merc. Perhaps we'll see each other again." Morgan smiled scornfully over her shoulder and left.

I was speechless. My head swam. Questions arose. Then, all at once, the pieces of the Dúl puzzle snapped into place. My temper flared.

"Merc—" Dúl said.

I pulled away from him. "No. Fucking. Way," I growled. Why hadn't I figured it out earlier? How he never referred to the king by name. *Too busy with his stupid voice and warm hugs. And his kiss.* "No wonder she was such a bitch to me."

"Please, let me explain."

"What's to explain, *my lord*? Or is it your majesty?"

Chapter 14

I crossed my arms in front of my chest and stood my ground in the center of the room. "You kiss me and then send me off to rescue your magic-slinging girlfriend? Were you planning to explain why you lied to me?" I noticed that I was shouting and clamped my lips together before I revealed any more about the effect these revelations were having on me. I was glad to be facing this on physically equal footing at least. It made me feel less vulnerable as the news sliced through my guts.

Dúl walked behind the desk, sat, and leaned back in his chair. Another, deeper sigh.

I told myself that I had to hear him out if I wanted my money. Sure, *that* was what kept me from storming out.

"First, I didn't lie to you. It's true that I'm king of the Shadow Court, but I never said I wasn't. I let you believe I was an underling because I thought you would be uncomfortable otherwise. Was I wrong?"

I glared. He nodded once.

"As for Morgan, she is not, as you call her, my 'girl-friend.' It's more complicated than that."

He scrubbed his face with his hands. This was yet another aspect of his personality—stressed and despairing. There had been glimpses of it, but I hadn't thought about what the cause might be.

"As the sovereign of this Court, I am expected to fulfill certain duties. One of those is to produce a full-blooded heir. Morgan was chosen as my counterpart in that duty. Neither of us was given a choice, and I at least am in no rush to embark on that particular journey."

"You're hoping to find a way out."

He nodded again.

"And that means, basically, she's not your girl-friend. She's your fiancée."

"She is extremely capable as my lieutenant and runs this Court better than I ever could. I respect her for that. We've known each other since childhood, so I care for her in a familial way, but that is the extent of my feelings for her. Am I being clear?"

"Sure, but does she know that? She was a straight-up nasty bitch."

"I can't speak about her emotions, but I have my suspicions."

Dúl had made sure to keep eye contact with me up to this point. Now his gaze dropped. He paused for a long moment.

"Those of us in the Dreaming age slowly, Merc. With the glacial pace of change, it can seem as though time in the Waking is moving faster, even when it's not. For a long time, I rarely left, engaging in border wars with my brother and leaving my Waking responsibilities under Morgan's care."

Before I could open my mouth to ask why he was telling me all this, he held a hand up and peered into my eyes again.

"When word of your early forays through the courts reached me, I ordered my ravens to observe you out of simple curiosity. A child who could shapeshift in such a unique way, who could get through three Courts virtually undetected—of course, I wanted to see how you would develop.

"I hadn't realized how much time had passed. The years seemed to breeze by. My network reported to me that Rebus had trained you into a formidable thief. Then stories of your exploits against the changeling underworld began to filter through my network. Your ability sounded incredible. I had to see for myself.

"I began to venture into the Waking more often. You began seeing that scum who, frankly, isn't good enough to serve as your doormat. I'll admit to being...jealous."

Without my permission, the corner of my mouth began to lift. I pretended to cough for an excuse to cover my smile. If Dúl noticed my grin, he hid it well.

"My moods when I returned to the Dreaming were mercurial. Unacceptable. Morgan called me out. We fought. She left. Shortly afterward, she disappeared, and here we are."

It all sank in. Somehow, I wasn't that surprised he'd been watching me for so long. I could see why someone in his position would want to keep an eye on my abilities. I could also see why he would have wanted to move in and snag my services before any more of his siblings caught on like Nemesis had.

"Didn't you realize I'd find out eventually? And if you're engaged to… why did you…? You let me think…" As soon as I spoke the words, I wasn't sure I wanted to know. A hasty exit suddenly seemed like a better idea. My skin began to tingle as if I were about to shift, and hadn't I just thought about shrinking down to the smallest possible creature I could imagine?

He cocked his head to the side for a moment, and then leaned his elbows on the desk, his lips resting on steepled fingers. He didn't answer. Instead, his intense gaze impaled me. I fought not to squirm. Deep in the recesses of my mind, I knew he couldn't give the answer I wanted. The answer that for so many reasons I had no right to want.

He got up and walked around the desk to lean against it. Taking my hand, he pulled me in front of him. My fingers remained in his grasp.

"I promised to tell you the truth, so before I do, are you prepared for it?" He ran his hand down my arm, pausing to squeeze my triceps.

Unable to get words past the dryness in my throat, I nodded.

He captured my other hand, and holding both in his, he said, "The truth is I would like you to join the

Shadow Court. Not merely as a subject. I want you to oversee the network. Be my Shadow Master."

"Master? That's been illegal for well over a hundred years." Could he hear the quiver in my voice?

He cleared his throat. Apparently, he got human humor because I could see that the corner of his lips twitched.

Stop watching his lips.

"I think you know what I'm asking. Your position in the Court would be second only to mine. You would be treated as my equal."

Whoa. Things just got much deeper than I thought I could handle.

"I...I'm flattered. But I just got a taste of the world... I want to see more of it. I don't want to be stuck somewhere for the rest of my life. I *can't.*"

He smiled. "I've watched you very closely, Merc. I know exactly what you need and what you want, even if you're not aware of it yet yourself." He pulled me a step closer. His tone dropped to a near whisper.

"As Shadow Master you'd travel the globe, engaging with all areas of the network. Your time at Court would be as limited as you like."

A thrill went through me. "Wh-what about Rebus and Nat? They're the only family I have—"

"You would gain a whole new family, but there's no reason you can't see your loved ones whenever you wish. The Manhattan office would be your base of operations. Live wherever you please."

"And this—" I pulled free and gestured from my

head to my feet. "Will I have to stick to one form so the network doesn't get confused? I mean I usually stay in one or two forms but—"

"Merc, you can run the court as a crow-headed dragon if you like. All I require is you." He stuttered. "You-your promise of loyalty to this Court. Everything else is your choice."

Dúl squeezed my arms again, working his way up to my shoulders. His face was a mask of calm, but his lips were the slightest bit tight. *He's worried I'll say no.*

It all sounded so perfect. Too perfect. There had to be some trick or loophole I wasn't seeing. What concerned me most was that I might be missing something because I didn't *want* to see. Because I wanted all of it. After a taste of the possibilities, I wanted more. It almost made me understand how—

"Paris."

More pressure, but then his hands stilled. A muscle at the hinge of Dúl's jaw convulsed. "Obviously, you have to do what you feel is best about him before making any long-term plans. Speaking of him, as an added incentive, your first order of business would be to eliminate the vampire threat. I would imagine your friend, Donny, would suffer greatly as a result."

If I'd needed magic words, he'd just said them. I had pushed out of my mind all I had seen at the pier, but I couldn't ignore it forever.

"What about Morgan? She hates me."

"I doubt that. But even if she did, she's a pragmatist.

She'll ultimately do what's best for the Court. There's one last piece. Two, actually."

I waited for him to continue.

He tugged me even closer, intertwining our hands and bringing them up between us. All of this was so surreal, but to have him touching me in such an intimate way was almost overwhelming. It was hard to focus on his words.

"I know there are memories you have been unable to retrieve about your past. I think I can help you recover them."

My eyes bulged. "How did you know?"

"Lord of hidden things. All part of the job." He smirked. "If you ever decide to uncover the mystery of your past, whether you join my Court or not, I will do everything I can to aid you."

His expression softened as he watched my mouth work like a fish's, no words coming out. I snatched my hands away and flung my arms around him, clutching him like a lifeline. "Thank you," I whispered. "That means a lot." I got a grip on myself and eased up on my chokehold.

My eyes misted. "My parents... my home... I hardly remember any of it. I don't even remember what or who I'm supposed to look like." A bitter laugh escaped my mouth. "For all I know I could be Martian green or some kind of fire-breathing monster."

He squinted at me for a second, but as soon as I caught his confused expression, it disappeared.

"Everyone deserves to know where they came

from, Merc. And, I admit, I'm quite intrigued to know your true face. I doubt it's anything less than breathtaking."

He brushed my cheek with his thumb. Holding me tightly, he leaned in. His mouth brushed mine, feather light. I should have pulled away. Images of Morgan and Paris flashed through my mind, but quickly burned out. As Dúl's lips fused with mine, I let him in, tasting the longing that had built over all the years he had watched over me. I returned his kiss, chasing all I had resisted since he came into my life. With each lingering moment, our bond strengthened.

There was no doubt about what he wanted from me and what he unconditionally offered. The question was, could I accept?

Chapter 15

Breathless and wobbly-kneed, I left Dúl's office. He seemed a bit tongue-tied too as he walked me down to the car. But he showed no qualms about massaging the back of my neck as we moved through the corridors.

One week. That was how long I gave myself to decide. I slid into the back seat and zoned out.

This was so bad. Emotions cycloned through me. The offer, the kiss, Paris...it all jumbled together in my mind. What a mess! And holy shit, Dúl was an incredible kisser. And I shouldn't have been thinking about that because, technically, I cheated on Paris. But *he* cheated first. And was using drugs again. And betrayed me by working for Donny.

Still, that didn't make my actions okay.

From that last phone call when we argued, deep down I suspected we might have been over, but I didn't want to deal with the likelihood. Now I had no choice. I fixed myself a shot of liquid courage—gin and ginger ale—for the trip home.

Around midnight, the driver dropped me at the bar.

As I opened the door, music blared. The place was full to bursting, a normal Saturday night crowd. The noise, smoke, and crush of bodies eased my nerves. I searched for Rebus or Nat but saw neither of them. On my way through the mob toward the back office, the part-time staff and a few customers waved or greeted me. This was home. Could I stand to go so far from it?

Rebus was sitting behind his desk, and Nat was reading over his shoulder. When I poked my head in, they looked up.

"Hey. I made it back in one piece."

Before I could say anything else, they rushed around the desk to hug me.

"What? Were you worried?"

We all laughed.

"You never know. Fullbloods, vampires..." Rebus said.

"About that..." We sat, and I told them everything that had happened, that I'd learned, and that I had been offered. They took turns checking on business and being filled in on the parts each had missed. We talked until it was near closing. By the time we were done, I mostly knew my decision.

One last thing would make up my mind one way or the other. I had to try, so I went back to my apartment and shifted to my female body in case he was home.

Paris was nowhere to be seen. I searched for positive thoughts. He could be working—sometimes he did security. Or he could have been doing something less respectable. Part of me wanted to reject the negative ideas out of sheer habit, but I couldn't ignore the truth any longer. Only nostalgia for what we'd had together motivated me to give him this one, last chance.

I lay in our neatly made, queen-sized bed watching the flat screen on the wall above the dresser. The sound was muted so I could hear when he entered the apartment.

He came home around dawn.

The front locks clicked, and the door creaked open. After it closed, there were two muffled thumps—his boots dropping onto the worn carpet. I listened and followed his path through the apartment—into the kitchen to find a nearly empty fridge. A bottle cap landed on the countertop. Footsteps padded through the living room. His belt buckle clinked, and I imagined him undoing it one-handed. Still unaware of my presence, he went into the bathroom and peed for an eternity.

Finally, he came into the bedroom. He had removed his shirt and left his fly undone. He stopped at the doorway. "Oh. You're back."

"Yes. I can tell how happy you are, but a party isn't necessary."

"You could have said hi."

I watched him closely. He didn't seem high or drunk. I breathed in deeply—sweat, faint mint, but from a distance, nothing to indicate more than his need for a shower.

"Where have you been?" I tried to keep my tone

neutral. It was hard considering he hadn't moved into the room. Any delusion that this might turn out well quickly disintegrated.

"Working. For *money*."

Funny. A guy who had only spent a couple of days with me completely ignored his "other half" to rush to my side and make sure I was okay. My adopted parents dropped everything to hold me because they were happy I got out of the Dreaming alive. Yet, the guy I had been in a relationship with for the past three years, shared my home and bed with for the past two, who I had been planning a future with, wasn't coming near me. Hadn't asked a simple how are you.

"That sounds great. What was the job?"

"Can't really say."

Well, if he was going to play *that* game... I hugged my knees to my chest. It felt like I needed a shield. "Were you working for Donny?"

He stared at me dumbly, which in itself should have been all the answer I needed. *Should* have been.

"Do I ask where you run off to when you're out saving the world? Or when you go who-the-fuck-knows-where with some fey boy?" He stomped over to the bed and jabbed the air in front of me. "I saw you, Merc! That night—it was just supposed to be you and the kid. But there you were running around with some dude. And then—"

"What do you mean 'was supposed to be?'"

"And then I find out you ran off with him! What the fuck was I supposed to think?"

How was he blaming this on me?

"Excuse me? You were supposed to think it was a job! Which it was!" I flew off the bed now, in his face. "A job paying me twenty Gs! Enough for us—" I gestured between him and me. "*Us*, you moron! We could have been out of here for good! My *job* was no excuse for you to let some vamp suck you dry. But that wasn't about hurt feelings or jealousy, was it? You just wanted some X." I shoved him backward.

Startled, he grabbed me by the upper arms, pivoted, and slammed my back against the wall outside the bedroom. "You ain't my fucking mother! I don't answer to you!" *Slam!* "You do what you want! So can I! Live with it or get the fuck out!"

He shook me again. My head knocked against the wall a third time. I swept both hands up between his forearms to break his hold then rammed the heel of my hand into his diaphragm. He doubled over, coughing.

He was trying to divert my attention, covering up his drug use and his betrayal and hoping I wouldn't notice.

"Paris, no matter what I feel now or felt for you before, you will *not* touch me like that again." I clasped one fist in the other to control the urge to wail on him. "Not anymore."

Snatching him by the hair, I leaned over and forced him to look into my eyes. "What did you have to do with Kendal?"

Paris's lips tightened. His eyes begged.

"Answer me!"

He rolled his eyes every which way.

I rattled his head, forcing him to focus. "What's the matter? You don't want to see what you've become? Are you afraid to see your reflection in my eyes—to see how low you've sunk?"

"Merc, come on. I just..." Tears and snot mingled along his top lip.

"Look at me!"

He deflated, sliding down the wall until his butt hit the floor.

Still gripping his hair, I roared. "What did you do?" Spit flew from my mouth. My skin burned to shift into something big and ferocious, but I held my form. "I could've destroyed you a hundred times over the past two years, but I always held back because this isn't you." Rage thrummed through me.

"Donny. *He* came to *me*, I swear. Found me finishing up a security shift one night." Paris's voice was choked. "I was clean before that, baby, I swear on my life. But he brought me a hit. I thought a little taste wouldn't hurt anything." He wiped an arm across his face.

"Then he starts talking about the Fringe and how bad it's getting." Paris shook all over. "He said if I helped him, I could make some good money. Get out of here. Go someplace nice."

I sniffed. Now that he was closer, I smelled the faint odor of vampire. What had I been thinking all this time?

After months of rehab and relapses, breakups and reconciliations, Donny had come along and wrecked it all with one little vial of red dust.

My heartbeat pounded in my ears, almost drowning out Paris's words. My blood boiled. For the first time since I was a kid, the shift started to take over, unbidden. Something rippled in my spine. I cried out. Squeezing my eyes shut and breathing deeply, I calmed enough to stop transforming.

"Why?" My voice rasped. "Why would you stab me in the back like that?"

Paris, his voice muffled, groaned. "I didn't think...I figured...get paid for bringing them to Donny, then you'd get paid for bringing the kids home. Double the money. No one was supposed to get hurt."

"Right. Because how much could it hurt me, getting knocked around in the dungeon? Couple of black eyes here, some bruises there. No big, right?" My voice cracked. "And what's a couple of innocent changelings? I can't... believe you. For so long, I've protected them, and you do this? And now, do you even know what he's done with the Courts? He's practically declared an all-out war with them!"

Donny was now first on my shit list, but this situation wasn't entirely his fault. If Paris gave in so easily, he hadn't been ready to quit. He never would be.

I had been fooling myself. "I'm out."

He didn't do or say anything to stop me while I packed my tools and clothes. As he lay on the bed shaking and watching me—not expecting any comfort and not receiving any—I retrieved the stash of money hidden in a panel I'd cut behind the TV. Paris's share floated down around him on the bed as I walked away from him for the last time.

Chapter 16

I moped around Rebus and Nat's apartment for the rest of the morning. Around midday, a package arrived by FedEx. Inside a bubble-wrap envelope was an ebony box with a beautiful raven carving on top. A note written in a spiky scrawl accompanied the box.

Merc,

Your true name and voice will open the box where you will find what I owe you. As for the other matter, when you have decided, enter the Dreaming and speak my name. One of my messengers will come to you.

Yours,

Dúl

Nat came into the living room. I sat on the brown microfiber couch while she sat on the floor opposite me with the scratched and water-stained coffee table between us. Two hundred crisp $100 bills filled the box. I started to count them, mostly because never in life had I seen so much cash, and I needed to touch it, to make sure it was real.

"You haven't said much since you showed up this morning. What's going through your head?" Nat said.

"Pfft...I don't even know. I keep thinking I should feel guilty about Paris. He's going to spiral out of control, and I feel like I should still be trying to save him from himself, but I know I can't."

"No one can say you didn't try your best."

"And then I think I should feel bad about kissing Dúl."

Nat scrutinized me. "If things were better with Paris—say, the way they were in the beginning—do you think you would have given Dúl a second glance?"

I shook my head and went back to counting. Anything to avoid her gaze.

Back when things were good with Paris and me, he was the only thing that existed for me outside of my work. Once the problems started, saving him from himself became my main purpose in life to the exclusion of everything else, including my family. My behavior had hurt Nat and Rebus deeply. He hadn't forgiven Paris. I hadn't forgiven myself.

"So, when do you plan to contact your king?"

A week later, a car picked me up from my new apartment in Yorktown Heights, about midway between my old family and new Shadow Court family. I had agonized over what to wear and decided not to look like I was trying too hard. I chose a new pair of skinny jeans, purple ankle boots, and a thick cable knit sweater.

Inside the office building, I rode the elevator up to the top floor but hesitated when the doors opened.

Morgan, wearing a fitted black suit and stilettos that were probably made by some designer I couldn't pronounce let alone afford, greeted me.

I wanted to jump down the elevator shaft.

"Welcome...Umbra."

The vision hit so fast, it startled me. "Oh, God. I remember."

My fingers and toes had gone numb from the cold, and I couldn't drag myself another step. There had been no food or water for days. I had fallen asleep behind a shed next to a cottage. Next thing I knew, Morgan was crouched next to me, smiling warmly.

"What's your name, little one?"

I had told her.

"Welcome, Umbra. You're safe here."

I *had* felt safe, unlike that other place with milder temperatures than the Summer Court that also felt like it didn't want me there. Morgan gave me her cloak—dark brown hide with a hood. My shifts had been frequent and mostly uncontrolled back then. She chuckled—*chuckled*—when I transformed into a miniature of her likeness.

Then we had reached the Shadow castle. There had been a large bedroom, a thick, midnight-blue robe, and a blazing fire. She'd ordered food for me. Servants waited on me hand and foot as I was fed and bathed. Then at one point, she started barking orders at the guards and screaming at one hunched woman. A slap rocked the servant's head back. The woman fell to the floor before slinking away.

The change in Morgan's demeanor freaked me out. The first chance I had, I bolted.

"Shall we?"

Now, in front of me, her gaze was as dark as a black hole.

"W-wait. Please, Morgan."

One perfectly shaped eyebrow lifted. Flawless, red lips pressed together. Annoyed? How hard was she biting her tongue at this moment? But was there also a trace of expectation?

"I remember. You. You helped me when I was in the Shadowlands as a child. I was freezing—starving—and you helped me."

The tiniest flicker of light flashed at me from deep in within the black hole and disappeared just as quickly.

She studied me for long seconds before responding and set her features to *practiced nonchalance.* "Yes. I'm not usually one to be taken with children, but you were especially pathetic. And your...antics, random as they were, amused me. So, yes, I took you in. Fed you. And then, like all ungrateful whelps, you disappeared without so much as a thank you or a backward glance. I searched for you, but I suppose you've always had a knack for escaping impossible situations."

The darkness deepened, and I could understand why. This woman, who doesn't seem to extend herself for anyone and always keeps the world at a distance, had let down that wall. And had gotten nothing for it but rejection.

"I was just a kid," I said quietly. "You were so kind to me. Gentle. But when I saw you flip and slap that old woman... Jeez, I was just a kid. It scared me, so I ran."

Another glimmer of something indefinable. A muscle in her jaw ticked. "Contrary to common belief, I am not some monster. I would never have *harmed* you, or any child for that matter. In fact, at the time, I had the fleeting thought..." She gazed past my shoulder as if the past were replaying on a screen behind me.

"Never mind what I thought. It was a long time ago. The fact is that 'old woman' had made a comment to another staff member about how high a price they could get for a 'pretty little thing' like you. I made it clear that you were under my protection. As you will come to learn, sometimes a woman in a position of power needs to remind her subordinates that she can wield a hammer as well as the finest needle. Remember that."

When I looked into her eyes, I thought they had taken on a glassy shine, but she blinked, and it was gone. Maybe my own sight was distorted by the stinging around my own lids. She'd tried to help me, and I had repaid her by making her look weak.

What might my life have been if I had stayed? Was Morgan thinking the same thing?

"I didn't know, Morgan. For what it's worth, I'm sorry I left the way I did. And thanks for saving me."

Her expression softened only a minute amount,

and that spark resurfaced. We would be working to-gether. Maybe over time we could become allies. Maybe something more, like friends.

"I...appreciate that, Umbra. As for my behavior the other day, let's say the duress of captivity put me out of sorts. My apologies. I am...pleased you've decided to stay with us. Shall we?"

Morgan turned and led me in silence to the "comfy office." *My office.* She didn't enter with me. As we parted, I noticed she still wore her trademark frown. It seemed to have a hint of sadness behind the usual anger.

Dúl sat behind the desk reading some papers. On the left corner of the desk, a small, black bottle sat next to a long, black feather. As the door clicked to shut us in together, he glanced up and smiled.

My pulse quickened.

"You've considered my offer."

Remaining by the door, I nodded. "Yes, but let's clarify a few things before I accept."

He gestured toward the empty chair. I crossed to it.

We sat together and hashed out details. He hadn't lied about granting me a ton of freedom. As long as I didn't work for any other fey, he had no problem with my outside "business."

That was an important detail for me, now more than ever. I intended to make Donny pay for what he'd done to Paris. To us.

Negotiations out of the way, I relaxed. "So, what's next? Do I sign somewhere, or...?"

He rose from his seat and stood in front of me. "There will be a ceremony where you swear fealty to me and to the Shadow Court. Likewise, I will promise to protect you, and the Shadow Network will vow to obey your commands...all very boring stuff."

I had to laugh. "Are you sure you don't want someone older? More experienced? I mean, heading the entire network...."

The corner of his lips curved upward, and he leaned forward. Running his fingers along one braid, he gave it a tug when he reached the end. His touch flipped a switch inside me, waking all my senses.

"My long-haired thief. I have never met anyone as talented or disciplined as you." He traced his thumb lightly along my jawline. "Anything you still need to learn, I'll gladly teach you, but you've already proven yourself capable of leading. You've even gained a couple of allies, from what I hear."

I felt as if all the air had been sucked out of the room. "This ceremony, I hope you don't expect me to kneel—"

His lips on mine stopped my words, feather soft at first until his restraint cracked. His tongue claimed mine. Heat raged through me. Before I could plunge my fingers into his midnight waves, he broke away.

He dipped his head and breathed out hard. Had I done something wrong? Dúl looked at me then, a tinge of red in his cheeks. Eyes locked on mine, his hands on the arms of the chair, he pushed my seat back and kneeled before me. Our faces were inches apart.

"You will kneel to no one. And if you will allow me, I would like to give you a gift."

I nodded.

His fingers stroked from the outer crease of my hips to my inner thighs to my knees. Gently he pushed them apart and positioned his body between them.

I had no idea what he had in mind, but my temperature spiked. My heartbeat raced.

With his finger, he traced the ridges and curves along the back of my hand, up the inner flesh of my wrist. I shivered.

My thighs tensed as my heels pressed against the chair legs, fighting the urge to snake around him.

He reached behind him to the desk, uncapped the bottle, and picked up the feather. Its tip looked evil, sharp. Dangerous.

"What—" I breathed.

"Shh...you may feel a slight pinch."

Dúl lifted my left hand, dipped the quill, and gently pierced my wrist. A dark tendril of shadow undulated from the feather and slithered into the tiny puncture. A shock ripped through me. I gasped.

He began to etch the ink into my skin. Each prick of the quill tip rippled pleasure through me. The shadows caressed every inch of me, radiating through to my very core.

As he gripped my hand to steady it, his pulse reverberated against my own, separate yet fluttering in sync. Two birds in frantic flight.

In my mind's eye, the image of two ravens, intertwined in a dive, awed me.

Another surge wracked me. I clutched the arm of the chair with my free hand as my back arched, the energy that filled me rising up through my chest, lifting me heavenward. It was almost more than I could stand.

I glimpsed Dúl through narrowed eyes. His breath came hard and fast. As his gaze locked on mine, his body jerked, and his eyes squeezed shut. I cried out.

The energy was too much to take. My frame shattered. I shifted fast between male and female, growing large with each surge of power, compressing back down in an attempt to contain the pleasure coursing through me. It was like my body wanted to experience the sensations in as many forms as possible while being aware that my wrist in Dúl's hand needed to remain still.

Finally, clinging to the vibrations swelling within me, I yielded completely, losing all sense of time.

One last burst of power filled me. My toes curled, fingers fisted, belly spasmed. With a great rush of breath, release. Bliss. My head lolled to the side. My eyelids grew heavy.

What in the Three Realms was that?

Dúl's chest heaved as he rested on his heels, back supported by the desk behind him. A sheen of sweat coated his flushed skin.

"So," I panted, "have you ever...?"

"Never."

"Any more gifts like that might lay us both out for a week."

"I'm for it if you are."

"Bring it. But feel free to take a minute. Looks like that took a lot out of you." I gave my king a smirk.

We both chuckled and smiled lazily at each other.

After a moment, he put down the quill and gingerly lifted my hand to show me his work. Black wings spanned from my thumb to pinkie when I spread my fingers; a tail fanned across my wrist. A bird's head and beak cut across my index and middle fingers. A raven. I loved it.

My entire body thrummed. My legs and arms quivered.

He grinned, still breathing as if he'd just run a race. "You now possess a piece of me—of my essence. I trust you'll recall a certain dagger Morgan had at the time of her rescue. Normally, it only responds to a pureblooded fey, but..."

The dagger was suddenly in his hand. Now silver, the blade gleamed. Fading from his palm, it appeared in mine. "My father gave the Shadow dagger to me. Now, it's yours."

The dagger's power flowed through me, electrifying every cell. My body felt as if it were expanding again. I felt inhumanly strong, yet I thought my legs might not support me.

"Try it."

From the chair, I flung it across the room. It spun and lodged in the wall. An inky web spread across the wall's surface. In a moment, the dagger appeared back in my hand.

"Wow." I was floating but exhausted.

He gently caught the fingers of my newly tattooed hand, leaned in, and brought his lips to my forehead.

I felt invincible.

"Thank you, *my lord*." I chuckled.

Dúl rolled his eyes, stood, and pulled me up against him. "Don't ever call me that again."

He kissed me, long and deeply. As we melded together, intense heat filled me, mingling with the Shadow energy. Where these kisses might lead, I had no idea. Even if they ended in heartbreak, I would ride this out. I couldn't wait to see what my shadows held for the future.

Chapter 17

My introduction to the Court took place over the course of two ceremonies. The first was relatively small. I was becoming fond of a body that incorporated my favorite features from both of my preferred bodies. Decked out like a true badass, I wore head-to-toe black leather, my hair flowing out, wild and free. In the auditorium of RavCorp, I met my Shadows—the members of my Shadow Network.

The second introduction, in the great throne room of the Shadow Castle, brought me in front of the entire Court. I was slightly intimidated until Dúl encouraged me to appear however I felt most comfortable. I showed up in a long, black gown and velvet tuxedo tails, but it was the feel of Dúl's warm skin against mine that soothed me when he lifted my hand, presenting me to his people. We mingled at the reception for a short time before retreating to his royal suite for the rest of the night.

After all the ceremony and traditions, I spent a few days recuperating in the Dreaming. A couple of nights later, Dúl wanted to give me my own apartment in the castle, but I wanted to hold off. It felt too awkward with Morgan in the opposite wing.

I used some of my time in the Dreaming to acquaint myself with my new powers. Hiding in shadows took on a much more literal meaning. It was a blast. But there was unfinished business to handle.

Aside from a new six-figure salary from RavCorp, my position as head of the Shadow Network held some sweet perks. Among the most useful were the ravens. Dozens of them could trail Donny. Having eyes everywhere was new and made life so much easier.

Within a couple of weeks, I knew all his movements —every girlfriend, every brothel, every illegal gambling spot. On a quiet night in early December, I struck.

Donny was married but had several mistresses aside from occasional one-night stands. True, he had money, and he had an okay body—short, stocky, muscular—but he also had a weird, pear-shaped head with a hairline that receded into a U that was still obvious even with his buzz cut. His eyes were beady, and he wore a full scruff of a beard to conceal a shapeless chin. Money has a blinding effect, I guess.

His wife was out with friends, and he had returned a little after midnight from one of the side women. The driver/bodyguard dropped him at the door of his five-thousand-square-foot mansion before taking the car around to the garage. Donny didn't notice that the shadow near the hinge side of the door extended a little father than was natural.

The lock clicked. I whacked him on the back of

the head before he knew I was there. His unconscious body landed in a heap at the top of the marble steps. I retreated into the darkness to wait for the bodyguard.

The thug hurried up the stairs with a shout when he saw his boss. As he tried to revive Donny, I sliced the side of his face with my Shadow dagger. Within a moment, he was clawing at his face and shouting, blinded by the dagger's magic. Having to drag the dead weight of the Mafioso's form was inconvenient, but the satisfaction of finally having him at my mercy was worth it.

With no desire to be turned to a block of ice if he woke up too soon, I bound his hands, feet, and mouth with special restraints Dúl had made specifically for dealing with the Winter Queen's spies. Then I dragged Donny to the car in the garage, thankful that the keys were on the seat, and drove him back to the Fringe.

The dungeon had been cleared out hours ago by the network—my Shadows—as had Donny's other holdings. Now it was just the two of us. I threw cold water in his face and slapped him a couple of times until he woke with a splutter.

"Wha-what the fuck?"

"Morning, sunshine."

He narrowed his eyes at me and began to thrash against his bindings. He was in a chair inside the cell I'd occupied so many times and not too long ago. "Let me out of here, or I swear—"

"You'll do what? Spit at me? Yell at me? Have someone beat the shit out of me? Help my ex-boyfriend get hooked on X again?" The last words came out on a growl.

Holding back my temper long enough to get the information I needed would be tough. Dúl offered me the Court interrogator, but I declined. This was personal.

"You have no leverage here, Donny-boy, so let's make this` easy. Tell me who's financing the vampires, and I possibly won't destroy your entire life."

"Fuck you, Merc. Nothin' you can do to me." A glob of mucus sailed through the cage bars.

"Thought you might say that." On the guard desk sat a closed laptop. After opening it, I brought it closer to the cell bars. He was tied to a metal chair where he could see clearly. "Each of these little boxes on the screen is one of your businesses. Except for this one down here." I pointed to the vampire's lab, which had not been cleared of occupants. "You recognize that one, don't you, Don?"

He sneered but remained silent.

"You answer me, and I don't blow them sky high one by one. If not...Najat?"

"Yes, Mistress?" she said into my earpiece.

The image in the upper left corner of the screen showed a brownstone building a couple of blocks in from the Mid-Hudson Bridge. A silent poof clouded the section of the screen as the building went up in flames.

"No! Goddamnit!"

"That was one of your whorehouses, wasn't it? Is

that where Paris hooked up with those vamp bitches a while back? Profitable one, from what I heard. Let's try again, an easier question. Who's the head of the vampire nation these days?"

"Ain't tellin' you shit! You can suck my—"

"Go ahead." The second building destroyed was a little log cabin he'd bought for his favorite mistress last year. He'd been there with her tonight. "She wasn't in there, but rest assured, I know exactly where she is."

The Poughkeepsie Fire Department and those of the surrounding areas had a busy night ahead. I felt a little guilty about that.

Donny held out for a long time, even after everything he had built went up in smoke and ash. I brought in a couple of ravens and let them peck at him as he refused to give up any information. He wasn't nearly as venomous once they got a taste for his eyes. Finally, he told me what he knew, which wasn't everything, but it was enough.

When I dismissed the ravens and opened the cell, a heap of shredded flesh sat before me that leaked glimmering white fluid from dozens of punctures. Not an ounce of sympathy stirred in my heart for the lowlife who had hurt so many lives.

One image remained on the screen—the warehouse.

"Thanks for the info, Donny. I wonder—would it be super cruel of me to leave you to explain to the vampires what happened? To force you to face such complete and utter desolation? Your life would totally suck out there."

His one good eye rolled in its socket and blazed in fury at me. Dozens of punctures oozed over his face.

"Take out the last one, Naj."

The warehouse exploded outward, metal twisting and bending in every direction. The inside became a bonfire, turning the night into a yellow, orange, and red chemically fueled sun. I smiled.

"Aaand there go your partners. Now...what to do with you?" All his fight was gone now. I crouched down in front of him. "We have a history, so I suppose I should let you off easy."

His eye glimmered with a shred of hope.

"But I won't."

I knocked him out again, transported him down to the burning warehouse, and left him bound near the wreckage with a note skewered to his arm.

Dear Bloodsuckers,
You can thank this guy for the destruction of your lab. I wouldn't let him get away with that if I were you. Your friend, Donny, also gave up the name of your boss. I'll be coming for him next.
Always watching,
M.

Epilogue

In the tallest tower of the Shadow Castle in the Dreaming, the king rested his elbows on the balcony's edge and peered over.

My king.

I let the door shut softly to let him know he wasn't alone and padded up behind him. My hands caressed his sides as I wrapped my arms around his waist and pressed in. I rubbed my cheek against the planes of his back, loving the contrast between the hard, muscular ripples and the soft silk of his charcoal gray robe. Breathing in his sweet, spicy scent, I sighed.

Dúl's fingers laced with mine. "You got a name?"

With a nod, I ducked under his arm to stand beside him. His lopsided smile drew my attention to his lips, lush and inviting. I couldn't wait to feel them traveling over every inch of my skin. "Chevalier. Serg Chevalier. He's the one. Like we suspected, the Fantine name was just a cover."

As he digested the information, I swept my gaze over the landscape. Hints of deep orange, blue, and purple outlined the horizon. Shadowy silhouettes looped and danced against a backdrop of muted blues and purples.

"And your other business?"

"Done."

Silently, Dúl hooked his arms behind my back and guided me to his bed, laying me down on a dusky gray duvet. Whatever body I was in, he liked when I wore my hair in two long plaits for him, and now he unbraided them, slowly, his eyes locked on mine. The tease. There was no rush.

A slow burn started in my belly, fueled each time he brushed against me. When my hair was wild and wavy, he plunged his fingers in, caressing my crown, over my shoulders, below my collarbone. I could tell by the glint in his gaze what he was remembering—the two of us intertwined, coming undone, together.

He eased me back against the pillows, fanning my curls out around me. He smoothed a stray strand from my cheek, trailed along my jaw and over my smile. My tongue peeked out, licked around his thumb before sucking it into my mouth. His eyes blazed. I could tease too.

"You'll stay the night?" The huskiness of his tone sent a ripple of heat coursing through me. No more playing around. Here, where it was always twilight, we could pretend we had all the time in the world.

I reached up, locked my hands behind his nape, and drew him down to me. *I wouldn't dream of being anywhere else.*

About the Author

Andrea Stanet's fiction has appeared in several anthologies, an online literary magazine, the *Nighlight Horror Podcast,* and most recently she released her first independent novella, *Spirit of the Wolf* on Amazon. Currently she is publishing serialized short stories under the *Anti-Villains* anthology on Laterpress and is the founder of Dragonlight Press. While she doesn't shy away from any genre, her passion is writing fantasy and horror fiction for various age groups.

Andrea spent thirteen years tutoring English and Essay Writing online. Her hobbies include studying the Korean language, reading, gaming, running, photography, and walking in the woods near her home. Andrea lives in New York with her husband, two kids, and two cats.

Social Media Contacts

Website: http://andreastanet.com
Facebook: https://www.facebook.com/
AndreaStanetauthor/
Twitter: https://twitter.com/AndreaStanet
Instagram: https://www.instagram.com/astanetau-
thor/
Goodreads: https://www.goodreads.com/author/
dashboard
Laterpress: https://antivillains-
anthology.laterpress.com/about-author

Other Work by Andrea Stanet

Spirit of the Wolf

Hey, Mom. Sorry to wake you. Really horny, can't sleep, boyfriend's trying to have sex with me, and I want to, but I'm not ready yet. Oh, and I might be falling for a girl I met. Goodnight!

College freshman, Asia, is having a rough time these days. She can't sleep and goes running in the woods at ridiculous hours. That's how she met Nati, her new friend. Asia also has a boyfriend, Jesse, who right now is being clingy and possessive. Something is not right with him, but she's losing patience. Besides, Nati is much nicer to be with. And seriously attractive.

Then there's the matter of her wolf spirit. She doesn't know it's there yet, but something else does. Nati's *Jaddi* sees it in her too. She'll need to discover who she really is. Soon. No matter how hard it might be. Because that something wants her, and it means to have her whether she likes it or not.

The only way Asia can save herself is to choose—
when secrets are revealed, and those she trusts suddenly have different faces, who will she become?

The spirit of the wolf may be all she can rely on.

Excerpt: Umbra's Winter

From her castle gate, the Ice Queen gazed into the snow-covered forest around her. All was silent except for the occasional howl of a wolf pack on the hunt for sustenance.

A disembodied voice hissed from the darkness. "He watches, your highness."

"Yes, Lemooria. His shadow floats over the land, undetected, or so he thinks. He isn't the only one who has command over the darkness. The Shadow Lord will learn that soon enough."

Pity. Of the others, Dúl had been the only one to show true promise and vision. The only one capable of the ruthlessness and focus necessary to achieve his ambitions.

The others allowed emotional ties and blood ties to bind them. Not the master of shadows. At least not until the shifter, with no memory of the past, had turned his head. Distracted him.

"And what of the shifter, highness? When will you reveal the truth?"

"Patience. Merc has a role to play too."

A sizeable role at that.

Merc's true origin would shock the irritating creature, causing such sorrow. How much would it hurt?

And how would the Shadow King respond when he learned about his beloved?

The queen couldn't suppress a smile that revealed sharp fangs. The fallout from her plan would be delicious.